The Summer Surf

Sue Carpenter

Sue Carpenter

Contents

The Road

'Freedom!' I scream out the window to any sheep that can hear me over my bleating music. This two-hour road trip is the longest I've ever driven alone – the first time I've done anything alone. Although, this road I know as well as anyone does. It's the only road out of Oneonepai, our small country town. My trusty old station wagon is winding around and through the native bush, leaving the farms and West Coast black sand beaches in the rear-view mirror.

In just over a month, I'll finish school. Terrifying. School is all I know. Everyone keeps asking me, 'What are you going to study, Sandra? What do you want to be when you grow up?'

How am I meant to know? All I've ever done is to be a student. There are so many jobs out there. So much choice. How am I meant to know what to do when I haven't tried them all?

I beep at Mrs Johnson; she must have finished her postal deliveries for the day. She returns a 'hello' honk from her van.

I don't know what I want to do in life, but I know what I want to do this summer. I'm trialling to be a lifesaver at Ngaruma, two hours south of the farm. Ngaruma is one of those small towns that explodes with people during the summer with a relaxed holiday vibe. Mum often says I could stand on a surfboard before I could walk, and I'd surfed through my childhood.

'Holiday,' I sing to a cow I pass who looks up at me, grass dangling out of her mouth.

My car shudders and pulls to the left. I'm shaken out of my deep thoughts about my non-existent future plans. A fence post whizzes past my door as my life flashes in front of my eyes. I've lost control of my car. Am I about to die? I can't die – I haven't even been kissed yet.

Almost skidding, I slow down and pull over. Whew! So far still alive. Maybe I should just kiss the next boy I see.

I jump out to check the car. I can already hear the air hissing out of my back right-hand tyre. Seriously, why now? At least the weather is nice.

I'm not a girlie girl who needs a guy to do things for her. But I am the baby of the family, and my brothers always take over from me. I know how to change a tyre – in theory.

Opening the boot to get the spare, I decide one thing: I'll not let this, or anything defeat me. I say it repeatedly! First thing I have to do is turn my hazard lights on.

I dash back in the car to put on my hazards, and when I get back out, a new blue station wagon with a surfboard on its roof racks is slowly pulling up behind me.

My mind is full of all those old ghost stories, a lady running out of petrol on the main road, or the unsolved murder TV programmes that Mum watches. I laugh at myself for being so dramatic.

We are a close family, although none of us look the same. Even the twins, Tony and Richard, who are eleven months older than me, don't look related to each other. I have brown hair. One twin, Tony, has brown hair, too, but his hair is fine. Mine is so bushy I have to tie it back most of the time. My oldest brother, James, is a redhead, and Chris and Richard are blonde. Our eyes are different, too. My eyes are blue, and some of my brothers' are blue, yet some are green.

Tony is the tallest in the family, and I'm taller than the other twin, Richard. Seriously, we are quite the eclectic mix.

That said, we all have toned bodies. We all lead active lifestyles. My oldest two brothers have been away at tech since they left school. James is going to be an electrician; Chris is going to be a builder. One twin was going to university to be a vet, and the other an artist, leaving no one home to help Mum and Dad with the farm.

It's not so much about the money for the summer, but my chance to get away. Surf lifesaving is hard to get into. They only take eighteen people. I have zero experience in anything like this, but Dad always says, *with a positive attitude, you are halfway there.*

There is only one person I want to reach out to. Grabbing my phone, I call my oldest brother James. 'Hey. Letting you know, I've

just driven past the right-leg turn and have
a flat tyre. It's under control. Telling you,
for safety reasons, some guy's pulled over
to help me.'

'Keep me on speaker,' James says.

When I get out of the car, I see the guy
who has stopped. He's not much older than
James, but a lot better-looking. He looks
totally kissable. Taller than me, and his
eyes are the colour of the waves I surfed
earlier.

I place my phone in the boot, making sure
the speaker is where James can hear me,
even though the guy doesn't seem to be
giving off any danger vibes right now.

'Hi, can I help you at all?' he asks, running
his left hand through his styled blond hair.

'I.... um.... flat tyre,' I stumble over my
words.

'Sweet. That's something I can help with.
Are you heading to the beach?' he asks,
looking towards the surfboard on the roof
of my old beat-up ute.

'Best place to go,' I say, checking out
his board. He has a white Son of Cobra –
Classic Twin. I want to touch it, but I won't
be that lame.

'For sure! There's something about the waves after a storm like yesterday,' he tells me.

'Especially in the morning,' we both say in unison – we laugh together too.

His laugh is subtle, but sounds genuine. 'I'm Cody,' he reaches out to shake my hand. His hand's warm in mine, igniting my stomach with fireworks.

My handsome stranger has a name. Cody! It suits him perfectly.

'Hi Cody, I'm Sandra.'

Our hands stay shaking for a lot longer than they should. I just don't want to let go. This is the closest I've ever been to handholding. How sad am I? I pull away from the handshake. My body feels like it has electric shocks pulsing through it, and it goes cold when his hand is out of reach.

As he puts the spare on, his arm muscles bulge as he uses them. I can't help but stare. He pauses and grins up at me. My face blushes at him as he catches me watching him work.

Sadly, it doesn't take too long for him to change the tyre. I could watch his toned body work all day.

'Do you know there's a fab break south from here?' I say, wanting to see how his board flies. I'd only been there a few times, and let's face it, it's not better than the beach where I'm heading, but I'm keen to spend more time with this beautiful stranger.

'I've time if you want a quick surf now,' he says, looking at his watch.

The missing person TV program pops back into my head.

Missing: Sandra Welch, 17.

Last seen on her way to surf lifesaving. Average height, bushy brown hair, and blue eyes.

It's ten in the morning. Sign-in for the trial is 3 pm, so I've got a few hours spare.

I'd wanted to get settled in and have a surf on the beach before signing in, but for Mr Handsome, believe me, I have time.

'Follow me,' I say, skipping back to the car. As soon as I close the door, I put the phone back on speaker.

'Are you still there?' I ask James.

'What on earth?' he laughs.

'Shut up,' I sink into my car seat.

'I am coming to the beach. I have to see this guy.'

'Go away,' I say, feeling my face burn again.

'I could see the fireworks from the chook shed, Sandra.'

'Stop teasing me!' I fanned my face to cool it.

'What's he look like?'

'What, does that matter?' Anger replaced the flush, still red.

'How do you feel about how he looks?' James won't let it go.

'He's adorable,' I finally admit, my embarrassment and discomfort turning into ooze in my stomach.

James's laugh is explosive.

'What's going on?' Dad asks in the background.

'Don't you dare! I'll tell Dad I walked in on you and Vanessa in the stables,' I threaten.

'Sandra had some car issues, but it's all sorted,' James says before he continues laughing.

'Where is she? I'm on my way.'

'No, she is sorted,' James says.

'I'm going,' I say, hanging up and putting my beach music mix back on. As I'm singing along to my music, I look in the rear-view mirror and can see the handsome surfer singing along to his music, too. I laugh and roll down my window, putting my hand out. I do a hang loose hand gesture.

He laughs and does one back to me.

Crab Bite

The beach is fifteen minutes south. We drive in convoy and arrive there in no time. The colour of the sky changes as we near the coast, reflecting the deeper blue of the ocean that lies just beyond the groves of toi toi and cabbage trees instead of the vast grass paddocks we passed earlier.

I'm already wearing my togs, as is he, so it's easy to get ready to surf. Although he looks like he belongs on the beach, his board's not been used in a while, so he quickly waxes it. I'd surfed already today, so I didn't need to wax. I start every day I can with a surf at the beach next to our farm.

The waves are great, and no one else is here, leaving the beach for us alone. We surf, and I melt into the rhythm of the ocean as I always do. His cobra has so much speed and turns with force and velocity. The few times we are close, we smile at each other. We ride for over an hour.

As we splash out of the waves, our bodies flop down in the dunes overlooking the beach, and I watch a family set up their picnic.

'Love your board,' I let slip.

'Yeah, Dad got it for me.' His smile drowns as he stares distantly to the waves.

We chat a little, then just sit smiling at each other and looking at the waves, sifting our hands through the black sand. His fingers are long, nails – perfectly manicured. Mine are all broken and a mess. My love of gardening gloveless kills any chance of having nails like his.

'I've got a big trial today,' I say, breaking the silence. 'I've been nervous, and this is the most relaxed I've felt in ages. Thanks for distracting me.'

'I've done nothing but study for months,' he says. 'It's nice just to get away.'

Ah, that's why his board hasn't been used for a while. 'It's nice talking to someone who's not asking me what I am doing with my future,' I add.

'Yes, let's not do that. What kind of trial? Can I help?' He turns from looking at the waves and looks only at me. I could swim in his ocean-green-blue eyes all day long.

My heart skips. Maybe my brothers aren't the reason I've never had a boyfriend. Maybe I'm single because none of the boys in our community have had this effect on me.

Composing myself, I answer him, 'I don't know. I'm going to run on the beach, swim in the water, that sort of trial. I'm not really sure what's expected of me.'

'On the beach? What kind of trial is it?' he asks.

'A surf lifesaving summer job.'

'Oh.' He gulps before his gaze is lost in the waves. 'Come.' He gives me his hand to help me up.

Our hands stay connected as we run to the water's edge. His hand brushes along the side of my thumb. Somehow, I don't combust.

'Stay here,' he says, letting go of my hand.

I stay, curling my toes in the sand, watching his lean body run up the beach, drawing a line on the sand every three metres before he runs back to me.

'What I want you to do is run to the first mark. Then back to here, and then the second mark, third mark.'

I run, turn, run, turn, run, turn. I'm energised. Running on the beach is what I'm born to do – it's where I most feel at home. If we'd run the school cross country on the beach, I would have won it every year, even beat the twins who are eleven months older than me, but we're the same year at school and I always place third after them.

Then he says, 'At the mark, try doing this,' and he shows me a smoother way to turn. 'Also,' he calls out over the waves, 'they have people who try to trick you into doing the same mark twice, so don't follow the leader; keep track of every turn.'

I run it again. With his new turning style, I shave thirty seconds off my first attempt.

'That's great.' He claps.

'Have you done it?'

'Yes,' he says. 'It's a lot of fun. But can you run?'

I take off, leaving him in my dust.

He tries to catch up. I don't slow down until I see a little boy crying at the water's edge.

Pulling to a quick stop, I change course and walk towards the boy, stopping a metre away from him, and crouch down to his level. 'Hi, are you hurt?'

'I got attacked by a cwab,' he sobs.

Cody catches up to me.

'Oh no,' I say, looking into the water and seeing a sharp stick dug into the sand, poking up where he thinks the crab is. The tide keeps swallowing the stick, then exposing it, repeatedly.

His mum runs over towards us.

'Hi, my name is Sandra,' I say to his mum. 'Your sweet little boy here hurt himself.'

'Thank you,' she says.

'I've got a spray in my bag that can help,' I say. 'Would you like me to get it?'

'Yes, please,' the little boy sobs.

I run up to my bag and get my mum's special tea tree spray out. I know half the battle with hurts is in the mind.

'This here is magic, so you can't tell anyone,' I whisper. 'It's pixie spray I got up in the enchanted mystery mountains. It helps cuts heal faster and hurt less. I'll put some on you now, if you like?'

He nods as I spray it on him. Wiping his tears off his face, he says, 'I already feel better.' His mother kisses her little boy's face and then thanks me for being so kind.

'You're welcome. See ya round.' I wink at the boy wrapped up in his mother's arms.

'Bye,' they call as we walk away. 'Thanks.'

Cody has been noticeably quiet. Together, we return to the peek-a-boo stick that the boy had scratched himself on and dig it out before someone else gets hurt on it. He says, 'I know we said no talking about the future, but teacher, nurse, and doctor all come to mind. You deserve to be a lifesaver.'

Heat burns my cheeks.

All our focus is on the stick and pulling it out of the ground, so we miss the gigantic wave upon us. We are both swept off our feet and knocked over, our bodies twisting till he's on top of me.

It's the most (and only) romantic moment of my life. As cold as the water is, where he touches me, I feel like I'm on fire.

He leans in like he's going to kiss me, but pauses above me. I can see him breathing. What's he thinking? Does he like me?

'This is one of those moments,' he finally says. 'Imagine if your tyre hadn't burst.'

'My tyre, oh my gosh, I have to go,' I say, panicking. I roll out from under him. 'I've got to get a new tyre and sign in.'

We get up and run past the little boy who has long forgotten his injury and is running around like a racing car. 'Beep beep.'

'Look,' I smile, pointing the boy out to Cody.

'You're good with kids.' Cody smiles back.

Would I never see him again? Our almost kiss magical moment. Our run has slowed to a walk again, and I yearned to spend more time with Cody. 'This has been amazing.' I beam at Cody as we reach our cars. 'Meeting a stranger, having an unforgettable hour, and dashing off again.'

'Will you leave me your sandal so I can find you again, Cinderella?' he jokes.

'Or we could meet for a run tomorrow morning?' I say. 'North beach at 6 a.m.?'

'Absolutely, I'll be there,' he raises his eyebrows.

I throw one of my sandals at him, knowing I've got another set in the car. 'You better meet me,' I say. 'I need that back.' With a wink, I get in the car and drive off.

Registration

Cody's in my car mirror for the next hour. I only lose sight of him when I pull into Ngaruma.

By the time my tyre's fixed at the only mechanic in town, I have an hour before registration, so I go to the beach. I'm kicking myself for how I'd been with Cody. Should I have done something more? Asked for his number? It's not always up to the guy, but I'm sure he has flirting experience, and I simply don't. Well, I have an experience with hot flushes now.

I park my car in the carpark and head straight to the waves. I practise running up and down the beach and doing burpees. The sand is softer to run on than it is at home, so I do different movements to adjust. I look over at the clubhouse, and it's packed. I guess I should head over. Good thing I do –

I'm one of the last to sign in at registration. I walk in, windswept and covered in sand. A girl with long blonde hair and even longer legs is wearing a short white skirt. She looks down her nose at me. Makeup piled on far too thick, yet she snickers at me.

It shocks me to see all the other girls in short summer dresses, makeup, and hair done perfectly. They all look ready for a party. I look ready for a shower.

Turns out, registration is just putting our names down, working out who will sleep where and in what teams, and getting settled in before an enormous meal and bonfire. Hence the clothes.

'Welcome.' A man stands on a platform to quiet the crowd. 'My name's Shane. I'm in charge of this week. There are so many of you, so this will all take a bit of working out.' He pauses. 'We'll put you in groups. Here are the six chosen leaders. They will come up and choose teams. Each leader will give you the lowdown on what's what and who's who.'

It's a lot to take in. I look around at the crowd, searching for a familiar face, but I can't. Too many. I'm outta my comfort zone for sure.

Shane continues, 'But first, I want to say all the best. There's over two hundred of you here, yet only space for eighteen. You will all stay tonight, and it will be cramped. Just put down your bedding wherever you find a space. Tomorrow, we will grade you all, and we will meet up. After that, sadly, over half of you will head home. So, from now till then, have fun, make friends, and show us what you've got. We will be watching. Enjoy!'

I decide to just have fun and gain experience. That doesn't mean I won't be giving it my all. The plan is to go hard. I always keep up with my brothers. I can keep up with this lot.

So many people are here. It's crazy.

'Jimmy, Meg, Ryder, Nina, Api, and Cody come on up. These guys are my eyes and ears,' he says. 'Go get your teams, leaders, and start orientation. See you in an hour for tea.'

Cody is here! And a leader. Cheeky sod. Why didn't he tell me? Cody makes a beeline for me, grabbing a tall, lanky guy with a brown afro and a red-haired girl on his way. He takes my hand and squeezes it with a let's-go wink. My hand throbs with his warmth still. I smile at him. No wonder he knew how to show me that stuff on the beach.

We follow him into a large hall which has windows on one side overlooking the beach. 'Hi guys, I am Cody; this is my third year here. I like to think I am approachable, so if you have questions, just come ask.'

'Far out. He's hot.' I hear a girl next to me say. She isn't wrong.

Cody continues to welcome us. 'First, everyone is rushing off to the best beds in the dorms, but unless anyone objects, I think we should all sleep here in the clubroom. It has the best view of the beach and loads of bathrooms.'

We set out our beds with a walking space between each mattress. The others start asking Cody questions. I lay out my sleeping bag, put my bag at my feet, and just sit on my bed watching the others.

My life's dominated by males, and I'm hoping to make some female friends, but I'm dressed like – and have only spoken to – guys so far. I sit in the middle of my makeshift bed, surrounded by boys. We chat about the surf at our favourite beaches. The buzz reminds me of bees back at the farm. I miss the farm but am embracing this different chaos.

Cody sneaks over to chat to Andrew, who I've been talking to the most. 'Sorry, I got interrupted. Do you mind if I swap mattresses with you?' he says. 'I need to be in the middle to monitor everyone.'

'Sure,' Andrew says, moving away.

'You okay, Sandra?'

'Yeah,' I say, 'I'm just recalling a conversation I had with a stranger today who knew things and purposely misled me.'

'Misled you? Ah, well, that's better than lying, I guess.' He has the cutest, cheekiest grin I had ever seen. Freaking adorable.

'At least I get my sandal back before tomorrow.'

'It's in my car. You will still have to wait,' he winks.

'My poor, exposed feet.' I can't help but laugh.

Other girls watch Cody talking to me. I'd be green if I were watching him chat with someone else. One gives me the evils, and another points at us talking and laughs.

Cody touches my left foot gently, sending a buzz through my body. 'They'll be reunited soon. Here is a pair of my socks in the meantime.' He takes out a clean pair of navy and white socks from his bag and places them in my hand.

'Not sure if that's sweet or gross.'

'Yeah, possibly both.'

'Excuse me, leader, where are the men's loos?' A guy interrupts us.

'The stick man is the boys,' Cody says, 'the stick wearing a skirt is the gals. Free time, guys. Go check the beach out. You've got forty mins, go.'

I hear a girl calling, 'Cody?'

'Hide me,' he says.

I laugh again. 'Big strong surf leader, scared of a girl?'

'That's not a girl,' he looks around, assessing the threat. 'You will see! Trust me.'

We run over the soft black sand towards the salt water with the guys from our group. My togs are still on under my clothes. Cody takes his tee off with ease.

The fancy-dressed girls sit on the beach and watch us. Refreshing waves crash into my body like a rush of energy. They always make me feel like this: stronger, re-energized.

I glance at the girl who's calling Cody. It's the blonde leader who looks like a beachside Barbie. The one who had snickered at me. She has my skin crawling. I'll have to watch my back around her.

'Most guys would run to her,' I say.

'She's a trick of nature, like when the insects attract their prey. I would rather camouflage and live another day.' He dives under the water.

I follow. We swim around after each other. There are twenty of us swimming, but Cody and I stick close, body-surfing the same waves. At the end of each wave, he gives me a hand up and our hands, like they had earlier, stay connected just a little longer than they need to.

I begrudgingly exit the waves, leaving him alone. Planning on putting effort into my appearance to help make a friend. It is then that the Barbie doll leader charges straight to me.

'Did you see where Cody went?' she snaps.

'Hi,' I say casually, 'sorry, who is Cody?'

'Your leader, the one you were talking to in the water.'

'Oh, that's right. No, sorry,' I say, then blurt out, 'I have a question,' desperately trying to think of a question to distract her. Cody is moving his way around her back and will run into her for sure.

So, I point in the other direction, 'Is there anywhere down there worth seeing? I'm thinking of going for a run tomorrow morning?'

She looks down at me again and scoffs, 'No idea.'

'Oh,' I say, 'sorry, I thought you were a leader – here to help.'

'I am, but I don't go running.' She rolls her eyes, clearly frustrated by me. Perfect.

'Ok, thanks,' I say after getting a thumbs up from Cody, who's disappearing out of sight into the club rooms. 'I think that Corey guy is out by the break.' I point into the water.

'His name is Cody,' she says. 'Corey is a girl's name.'

'Oh,' I say, but I'm genuinely surprised this time. I've only ever known guys called Corey. I head back to the clubhouse to freshen up.

Dressed in a clean yellow and white daisy dress, I enjoy dinner. Hamburgers and fries. I try to eat it like a lady and only get a small amount of tomato sauce on my dress. Thankfully, I meet a few girls.

A familiar round face hidden behind a mop of brown hair approaches me. 'Sandra Welch – alone?'

There are two hundred of us, but I know what he means. No siblings. It's rare to see any Welch's alone with the five of us similar in age.

'Hey Zach,' I say. He's the twins' friend from my class. He and I chat for a bit. I'm pretty quiet at school, so I don't talk to him much there, but he's interesting, and it's nice to have a little taste of home here. He would know me as the Welch girl, the undatable girl because my brothers are so protective over me. I don't talk to him too long.

After tea, we have a bonfire. Guitars, sing-a-longs, and roaring laughter. By my third yawn, I decide to obey my body and head to bed.

Cody's playing his guitar with a white-haired leader who looks like he's trying to grow a goatee. I watch their body language; they look close. They must have been mates for a while.

Inside the dorm, I go to the bathroom and have a shower, brush my teeth and all that human end-of-the-day stuff. As I leave the bathroom, I walk in on Cody and his guitar-playing mate talking alone. Their backs are to me in the seated area in the hall.

'Don't break up with her till Sunday. It will get turned into a weekend-long drama. Please, bro. For me?'

'We aren't together anymore. Why would I have to break up with her?' Cody says, sounding frustrated. 'I haven't seen her in ten months. If I were still dating her, we would've chatted, seen each other. Surely, she hasn't thought we were together all year.'

'Yes, she thinks you two are an item. Her room has framed photos of you. She's always talking about her boyfriend, Cody. Would it be so bad to date her?'

'Yes!' Cody yells. 'Would you want a girlfriend like that?'

'She's not that bad.'

'Help me avoid her. If I talk to her, I'll tell her we are not a couple when she corners me.'

'Wait till Sunday, please,' the white goatee guy pleads. I shift sideways to let him pass, muttering under his breath as he stalks out of the room.

'Hey,' I say.

'Hey,' Cody smiles, 'thanks for saving me before. Psycho ex.'

'And that guy?' I ask, seeing the other guy glance our way before disappearing.

'Her brother, but also my best mate.'

'Oh, that makes sense,' I fidget with the hem of my pink tee shirt, which I am wearing as PJ's for the night.

His eyes light up with a smile. 'You looked beautiful tonight, but I prefer the surf-swept version of you from earlier.' He grins.

I sit on my makeshift bed and put his socks on my feet. 'I have a date in the morning, so I need an early night.' I wink at him. 'Oh, a date, is it?' his eyebrows raise. 'Perfect, me too.'

Once Cody has checked on our group and settled them, he lays down next to me. Neither of us talk, but we don't look away either.

The psycho ex comes again and thinks Cody is sleeping, so thankfully, she leaves. I watch Cody's lips let out his breath as she closes the door. Is he really scared of her? I think I am. She has that don't mess with me look, and paired with her snickers, I will go out of my way to avoid her.

The last thing I remember before going to sleep are butterflies in my tummy as his feet skim close to mine. It's also the first thing I feel the next morning.

As I open my eyes, Cody is in front of me, his eyes already open in the pale pre-dawn light.

'Morning,' he whispers. He reaches out and sweeps some of my wayward hair from my face.

'Morning,' I whisper back, my insides buzzing as I think of the perfect way to start our morning. 'Wanna go for a run?'

His reply is a broad smile that melts my insides and makes getting out of bed the easiest thing in the world.

Thankfully, he and I are the only two people awake. I quietly walk around sleeping bodies and freshen up before meeting Cody out front for our run. The beach is as empty as the chook food bowl the day after my brother forgot to feed them. We run down the beach for

30 minutes and 20 minutes back up, the sunrise painting the clouds and dunes with light.

I pause and ask Cody, 'What's the dress code today? I keep getting it wrong.'

'Only for the girls,' he laughs. 'It's beach shorts always for us guys.'

'That's how I like it,' I admit.

'We do, too. The girls spend ages putting their makeup on, and it just washes off,' Cody laughs.

'I know. That's crazy. It's going to be a scorcher.'

Cody's goatee friend runs towards us. 'Hi,' he points at me, 'are you a runner too?'

'I'm used to horse riding in the morning but will run whenever I can here.'

'You think you will last until tomorrow?' he winks.

'No, I would rather not expect it and be surprised than expect it and be disappointed. I'm Sandra,' I say, shaking his hand. 'Any hints on how to stay here for tomorrow?'

'Hi Sandra, I'm Ryder, one of the leaders. I guess you've met Cody here. Just focus on your tasks. Lots of people get caught up in socialising and miss their chance because of that, but I noted you went to bed early, and you are training now, so I guess you have the right attitude.'

'Thanks,' I say, dragging my feet through the sand softly.

'We need to set up, Cody,' he looks at the lifesaving tower. 'You and Api are on first aid. Nina and Jimmy are on the beach, and Meg and I are in the water. I think something is going on with Meg and Api,' he says with another wink.

After breakfast, we meet in the clubhouse, no sight of mattresses on the floor, all our gear stored away in a cupboard. After a quick speech, we break into six groups. Three groups of boys only, and three of girls. Zach wishes me good luck. I smile in return. My group leader is Meg. She tells us this is her fourth year, and she impresses me by learning our names and making conversation with us all. We team up with Ryder's group and start in the water.

First, there is a series of water tasks – swimming around buoys and racing each other in from the break. I splash away in the front of the pack. Diving under the crashers and circling buoys, I'm happy with what I achieve as I pass Zach; he is a good surfer but seems to struggle. He isn't the only one struggling. A lot of the others cannot do some tasks.

'Great job, Sandra,' Meg says when she leaves the water.

Then, we swap stations and do beach tasks. My group is the last to do the trials. It is the running and turning challenge I'd learnt at the other beach. I replay the tips from Cody in my mind, watching as others screw up their turns. Zach had been the fastest in his group, but as I get my turn, I leave everyone in my sandy dust.

I look up and see Cody watching me from the clubhouse. He gives me a thumbs-up; I smile.

'Do you know him?' Nina asks me.

'No,' I say, 'does he not do that to everyone?' and on cue, he does it to someone else. He must know.

We have an hour-long break at lunchtime, and I chat to Katie. She and I walk to the local shops. Her red hair is pulled back – most of us girls' hair is – but I bet it won't be tonight if we get to stay. I worry that if I get through to the next stage, everybody will be dressed up again for dinner, and I only have one nice outfit which I've already worn.

The shop has a great selection of dresses and some rather horrid ones. It even has high-heeled sandals. We both try them, laughing constantly. I buy myself a pretty pair of flat red sandals and a red dress with my pocket money. I hope to have the chance to wear them.

I don't know why I want to impress Cody, but I definitely can't help but look for where he is.

I'm not the only one looking, either. Aside from his ex, who's always looking at him, or for him, most of the girls check him out, and Ryder, too.

After lunch, I have first aid. We get to do CPR. Cody tells everyone the story of me at the beach yesterday, but he says his friend and doesn't name me. He explains that talking to kids in a kind manner is just as important as how you help them.

Before we know it, it's 3 p.m.—time to go home if we haven't made it. My stomach turns. I want to work here so badly, and I'm not ready to give up this dream so soon.

Meg and Cody are impressed, but the ex doesn't like me. Will she stop me from making it? As we stand there, Cody smiles at me, but beside him, Nina glares at me with daggers of hate.

The leaders each choose fifteen recruits to stay another day. Meg starts.

'Sandra, Petra, Rebecca...'

She chose me in her first spot!

Ninety of us are selected, plus the six leaders. Still, so many will leave unhappy tomorrow. Katie, whom I had shopped with, is headed home. I almost had a friend.

Arms first, I slide my new dress on in the bathroom. Another girl from my group, Rebecca, is in the toilets putting makeup on.

'Hi, can you please show me how to do that?' I ask.

'Put make-up on?' Rebecca smiles.

'My mum never wears it, and I only have brothers,' I admit.

'Oh yes! You need to know this!' She opens up a bag and holds up bottles and tubes. Too many lotions, I can't keep up. She says words like base coat and foundation. It is confusing, but then, in front of the mirror, she adds some gunk to my skin, and magically, my face becomes more feminine.

'This is amazing, thank you.'

'Any time.' She puts all her potions away again.

Together, we walk out to the main hall, where Ryder and Cody are there alone.

Cody stops talking and blinks when he sees me. He looks like he's fighting a smile. Do I have lipstick on my teeth? I run my tongue along my teeth in case. 'Sandra, you don't need that stuff to look beautiful.'

'Do you know them?' Rebecca asks under her breath.

'Sure, Cody and I go way back...to yesterday.'

They all laugh.

'I've never worn make-up. Why not try it,' I say. 'This weekend is all about new experiences.'

'It suits you,' Ryder laughs.

'Come, sit with us for a bit.' Cody pats the ground beside him.

How could I not? The four of us make small talk for a while. Ryder is flirting with Rebecca, and he has his arm around her.

As they start kissing, Cody puts his palm up to my face and then slides the back of his hand down it.

'You are so very beautiful,' he says.

'I thought you said you don't like girls in makeup, yet you say this when I have it on?' I question.

'You are stunning with or without it. I prefer you without it because this way, everyone is going to look at you, and they don't know how much more there is.'

'Neither do you,' I say.

He laughs. 'No, not yet, but I know there's a lot more than just a beautiful face and hot body.'

I feel my face heat up.

He touches my face again, but this time with his fingers. As he leans in towards me, there's the echo of footsteps coming our way.

He moves away from me, as Ryder does from Rebecca.

Three boys from our group come in from swimming, get dressed, and grab their gear before heading off to the bunk rooms.

'Want to still sleep here tonight?' Cody asks me.

I nod, smiling.

Will I get my first kiss tonight? I move my bed to where it was last night, as does Cody. Ryder moves from his bed to join Cody. Rebecca is now lying on top of Ryder, kissing him again.

It's just the four of us inside, and it feels so awkward sitting next to them while they're going for it. The kissing sounds broken by the odd explosion of yahooing outside.

'Want to play darts?' Cody asks me.

'Sure, are you a good darts teacher?' I ask him.

Cody stands up and reaches his hand out for me. I take it, and still hand-in-hand, we walk over to the dartboard.

Once there, he lets go of my hand and pulls out a key to unlock the darts cabinet.

Then he takes out six darts. He hands me three pink ones, and he slides behind me.

'It's all about balance and aim.' He has one hand on my left hip and the other on my right arm. He's so close, I can smell his cologne, fresh linen mixed with salt.

'You smell nice,' I whisper.

'You smell amazing. Like saltwater.'

His lips are beside my neck, and I feel all the hairs stand on end. I want to turn around and kiss him, but he is the one with experience. If he wants to kiss me, I trust he will make the first move.

He helps me throw a dart, but it bounces off and doesn't even stick on the board. We laugh, and the others pull apart to look up at us before they go back to kissing. We go back to the longest lead-up to a kiss ever.

After I miss my first three darts, Cody shows me how it's done with his throws. He gets a bull's eye, and I cheer him on.

Then I have a turn without him, sending electric shocks up and down my body. I score 180.

'Bugger, I missed the bull's eye,' I say.

'You! What game are you playing?' he says, laughing.

'Ryder, look what Sandra did!' he calls out.

'Is that bad?' I ask.

'What the efff?' Ryder says, walking over, still holding Rebecca by the hand.

'Is that good?' Rebecca asks.

'Cody just taught me,' I say, and then I wink at Ryder.

Ryder cracks up.

'Do it again, and I'll buy you a surprise,' Cody promises, pulling the pink darts out of the board.

'I'll try,' I say.

Again, when Cody isn't looking, I wink at the others. Ryder laughs more. I throw my first dart. Sixty.

My second. Sixty.

My last. Sixty.

'What are you going to buy for her?' Rebecca laughs.

'Remind me never to play darts against her again,' Cody grins. 'But I'll play on the same teams with her – for sure.'

The four of us go for a walk down to the main shops. There is a dairy open that sells all sorts of things. I look at a bucket and spade. What crazy thing will he get me?

'No looking, you,' Cody says as he and Ryder walk into the shop.

Rebecca and I head to the beach and wait in the sand.

'Ryder is so cute! Do you like Cody?'

'Of course,' I say, blushing. 'We keep almost having moments, and then we don't. I am so confused by him.'

'He's been watching you all day. He definitely likes you.'

'Well, hopefully, I get in so I can see him more.' Without thinking, I make a sandcastle in the sand, then realise it's childish, so destroy it with my legs, my toes raking the sand down again.

'I really want this too. Tell me what you did with the darts.'

'I have four older brothers. We live on a farm, nowhere near anything. On rainy days and evenings, we play darts. I just scored the top score.'

'Well played,' she says as the boys arrive back.

'Close your eyes,' Cody says.

I feel him put a necklace on me. He kisses the back of my neck as he does the hookup. Next, he puts something around my wrist and kisses that, too.

'Can I open my eyes yet?' I ask.

'Yes,' he whispers.

As I do, he is right in front of me.

'The last thing I want at the moment is a girlfriend. I don't like drama, but you... I like.'

Our noses are almost touching.

'Do you think I am dramatic?' I ask him.

'No, I think you are perfect.' He steps back from me.

Another not kiss.

'Do you like them?' he asks. I look down at my wrist. There is a blue and green plaited friendship bracelet tied on it. 'The colours of the ocean and our eyes.'

I pull my hand up to my necklace. There is a surfboard hanging off a leather strap.

'Thanks so much. I love them.' I smile.

'You're welcome,' he reaches his hand out to me, and we walk down the beach holding hands.

Ryder has lifted Rebecca and is carrying her on his back.

We are almost back at the clubhouse, and Ryder leads Rebecca off into the dunes.

Cody drops my hand, and we walk over to the bonfire.

I sit next to Zach while Cody speaks to a group of people.

'Hey Sandra, you look amazing. I can't believe you are here without brothers threatening all the guys away.'

'Are they really that bad?' I laugh.

He nods.

Cody comes over and sits next to me.

'Will you please come to graduation with me as my date?' Zach asks.

Cody turns his head towards me. His arm slips behind my back, and he subtly holds me.

'I'll go with you as a friend. There is a chance I may be seeing someone,' I say.

'What do you mean, chance?'

'If a guy holds my hand, does it mean he likes me?' I ask Zach.

I feel Cody's hand move up and down my back.

'A guy from home?' he asks.

'No, and don't tell the twins.'

'As long as you don't tell them I hit on you.'

'Is that what you were doing?' I ask.

Again, I feel Cody's hand go up and down my back.

Nina crawls over the space and sits between Cody's legs. 'Hey you, where have you been?'

'Around,' Cody says.

'I don't like not knowing where you are. It's almost like you are avoiding me.'

Again, Cody has his hand go up and down my back.

'Zach, I'm going to bed. I want to get this summer job and need to be at the top of my game tomorrow. Night.'

'Good night, Ms Welch. Enjoy the book you are about to sneak away to read,' Zach laughs.

As I enter the clubhouse, Rebecca grabs my hand and pulls me into the ladies.

'OMG! Ryder is so good. He's going to vote for me to stay. Has Cody kissed you?'

'No, but Nina is currently sitting between his legs, falling all over him.'

'Oh, sorry,' she pats my back in support.

When we come back out, Cody is playing cards with Ryder. They go silent upon our arrival, so they must have been talking about us, too.

Cody is colder towards me now. He doesn't touch me at all, even though the other two are all over each other. The four of us hang out in the clubroom playing cards and other games. We stay up late chatting until Ryder and Rebecca disappear. Will I get that kiss finally? Nope!

'Cody,' that snarky voice calls.

Cody's eyes open in panic, and he runs to hide in a cupboard just before Nina enters the room. I push my lips together to stop a laugh. The measures Cody goes to avoid her. Sadly, he also has avoided kissing me again.

She stays for about fifteen long, painful minutes, questioning me about Cody. 'Where is he? When did you last see him? I wonder when he will be back – maybe he's sleeping somewhere else.' She tuts and checks her watch. 'I'll just keep looking.' When Cody comes back out of the cupboard, Ryder and Rebecca are back. We sit in the dark, talking about surf, sand, and beaches around the region.

Cody is close to me. I can feel him breathing and his arms close behind my back, but we are not touching at all. And we have still not bloody well kissed.

Reconnect

I watch the amber sun rise on the last morning of the trial as a group of us go for a run. Rebecca is struggling in the heat, so I slowly jog beside her. Her body curves in the right places, but she is nowhere as fit as I am.

We do the same tasks as before, with another cut coming mid-morning.

I can't catch a break with making friends. Although I make it, Rebecca goes home. My heart feels heavy that Rebecca is leaving. I haven't known her long, but I had hoped we would go through together – double dating the guys. I hug her, and she tells me she has a backup job and isn't upset. We exchange numbers, and she makes out with Ryder as he walks her to her car.

There are only thirty-four of us left now. We do more running exercises before they test us mentally by asking lots of questions in the clubhouse, like how we would handle a drunk or a homeless person and what we would do if it rained during our shift. I'm proud of my accomplishments, even if I don't get in.

In the end, the leaders put their top five names down. The people who get six are in, then five in and so on, until all eighteen spots are filled.

The leader coughs to get everyone's attention and starts. 'If you don't hear your name, please pack up. We hope that you learnt something and made some fabulous memories. Congratulations to Petra, Rose, Api, Alex, Ariana, Sandra...' The rest of the names blur into one. I made it. I'm in! My first summer job! I'll get to see more of Cody.

'You will join our six leaders. Congrats again,' Shane finishes with a smile.

There are still some girls, just not Katie and Rebecca, who I wish had made it. I came here to get experience and female friends, not to meet boys. Even my best friend back home is a boy.

It's now 3 p.m. time for the rest of us to head home with a letter explaining our job and a bunch of forms to fill out. I'll get home in time for Sunday roast dinner.

Everyone heads in to get their gear. As I grab mine, I see that there's a note in my bag.

Here's your glass slipper beautiful, see you in 4 weeks xxx

I grab my bag and bounce to the car, stopping when there's a high-pitched scream. I turn toward the drama and see Cody being yelled at and hit by Nina. Ryder runs over to break it up. I want to run over, too, but Ryder defuses the situation quickly.

Cody throws his bag over his shoulder and storms to his car.

We reach our cars at the same time. His is the flashiest one here; mine is the rustiest. We both head north, but I don't know if he even sees me. I try to catch his gaze to wave, but he's not looking up at anyone.

I drive behind Cody, and after ten minutes, I beep at him, and he pulls into a rest stop.

'Are you okay?' I ask.

He says nothing but paces up and down the gravel.

'I don't think Nina is your number one fan at the moment.'

'She has trouble distinguishing reality from dreamland,' he finally spits.

I don't know how to calm him down, but I have to try. I reach out for him, and he steps into a hug. 'Well, I guess you have something to look forward to in four weeks, sorting out whatever that was.'

'I have exams,' he says. He's taking short, sharp breaths still, so I rub my hands on his back to help calm him. 'I won't think about her again till I am back here unless I'm thinking of ways to avoid her.' He's starting to breathe more evenly now, and I lean back to check his face. 'I may sneak in a thought of someone else if I get a chance.' He smiles, looking at me with the shadow of a twinkle coming back into his eyes again.

'You're a flirt and a heartbreaker,' I tease him.

He holds both my hands, leans in, and slowly kisses my forehead. 'I'm so glad you got the job, Sandra.'

'Thanks for the tips. They helped.'

'You didn't need them. You'll be amazing. I'll try to get you on my team. I can't wait to see what else you can do, but I better go. I've got a long drive.' He gently touches my nose, smiling.

Back in my car, I carry on following him for a while until the road forks. We beep at each other and drive our own way.

The next month is slow. Graduation. More, *what are you going to do with your life?* questions. I can't wait to get back to the beach. When the day finally comes, I leave home at the same time as before. I drive to the beach Cody and I stopped at a month earlier.

It's a perfect surprise to see Cody's here, too. He's waving and smirking at me from the break.

I grab my board and paddle out.

He waves and winks at me.

'It's perfect.' I call over the crashing waves at the surf conditions, but I have no idea if he heard me. We surf for an hour together until we finally come to shore exhausted and lie in the warm dunes at the same spot as last time. The weather being warmer means there are more people today than there were a month ago. In a few weeks, like the other beaches, this one will be packed.

'You look great,' he finally says. 'How's your month been?'

'I officially have no future,' I say to him.

He teases, 'Are you just going to surf every day? Can you make a career out of that?'

'No,' I laugh, sweeping the excess salt water out of my braid. My hair is plaited, so I don't look wind-swept – it's the thought that counts.

'What do you like to do?' he asks. We are lying on the beach, just looking at each other, not touching, but there is a connection between us. Well, I feel it. Does he?

'Gardening, cooking, caring for our animals and neighbours' kids, art, all the creative things,' I say. 'I enrolled in a gardening course on Wednesdays and a cooking one on Thursdays, so I'll crash at my brother's place Wednesday nights in the city.'

'See, that's something – you managed to make plans,' he says. 'I live in the city.

Maybe we can catch up a few Wednesday nights?'

'I suppose that could be a plan.' I smile outwardly, but internally, I am floating in delight. 'In a year or two, one of my brothers will be back so they can help with the farm, but I think I'll stay on the farm till then.'

'I can't imagine living on a farm,' he says.

'Where do you live?' I ask.

'In an apartment by the hospital.'

'I can't imagine living in a box.' I draw a box with lots of windows in the sand.

'I've missed you,' Cody says out of the blue.

'You don't even know me.' I'm sure I blush a little. I add a tree to my sand art and then dots around the base as chickens, sheep, cows, trees, and flowers. I crawl on the sand as I draw the lines and shades till it is a farm with one tall, bland building in the middle.

'I feel like I know you,' he says, 'and I want to discover more. I love how you're somehow innocent and blunt in a caring way, and wow, look at the way you can draw a cow.'

In our month apart, I'd thought about him a lot.

He takes my hands. Electricity fires up between us again.

'Did you go out with Zach?' he asks, kicking at the sand.

'Kinda – we went to the graduation dinner together.'

'Did you hold his hand?' he asks, gripping my hands tighter.

'He tried to, but it's not like when you do. He's just a friend.'

A big smile flashes across Cody's face. Then, with his hand, he reaches out and touches my necklace. 'You still have this; do you like it?'

'I love it. I have worn it every day.'

He runs his fingers down my arm to my friendship bracelet. And, as he brushes his fingertips past it, he laughs, seeing how worn it's looking.

'What have you put this through?'

'Surfing, farm work, dishes.'

He's back to holding both my hands and leans in closer to me again.

'We better go. I want to get you into my group so that we can get to know each other even better,' he says, slowly licking his lips.

'And make sure Nina is not in our group,' I laugh.

'Don't remind me,' he groans. 'But seriously, we need to go,' he says. 'If we are in the same group, we get the same days off. This place is an hour's drive away. Do you want to come here for a day when we have time off?'

He stands up, taking me with him. We both have a board in one hand, but we're holding hands in the middle.

Anyone watching us will think we're a couple. It feels like it.

Sadly, we reach our cars, help each other load our boards, and are back to holding hands again. Cody walks me to my car door.

He slides his hands to my waist and says, 'You and I are going to have a magical summer together, I promise,' then he kisses the tip of my nose and jogs off to his car.

Returned

We arrive at the surf club just before two pm.

Nina and Petra are chatting outside. They show me where to park, and as they do, Cody drives in and parks his car a few down from me.

Nina comes up to me. She has one eye on Cody's car as she asks me, 'What's your name again?'

'Sandra,' I reply.

'Why is it you always look like you just got out of the ocean? Where do you live?'

'On a farm,' I say.

She crinkles her nose. 'Sandra, I think you are my roommate.'

No, no, no, no! 'Really, I guess we will get to know each other better then.' I use all my strength to show a smile.

'We can change rooms,' Petra tells me, rolling her eyes. Petra never hides her distaste for Nina. Nina never notices.

'Ok,' I say in a neither here –nor-there manner, but internally freaking out. I need to work on my poker face for moments like this.

'Cody!' Nina runs off as Cody hops out of his car.

'You need to watch Nina,' Petra says. 'she's going through a break-up. They were together for years.'

'Really?' I question.

'Yeah, she's really upset, but she thinks they will get back together.'

'I don't know. Looks to me like he's avoiding her,' I say as Cody tries to hide behind a nikau tree, unsuccessfully.

'You may be right.'

As I head up to the girl's dorms, I slip past Cody and Nina talking.

Unseen to Nina, I supportively touch Cody's back. He's all tight again.

'Please give me space,' Cody says to Nina, 'We. Are. Not. Together.'

'Yes, but we should be,' Nina sulks, reaching out for him. 'I'll give you space for a bit,' she finally agrees. 'We have all summer to sort this out.'

'We are not together, Nina. The past is the past.' He shakes her off.

'It's our future I look forward to,' she smirks.

'No, Nina.' Cody turns and walks away from her.

Nina calls behind him, 'after what we have experienced together we need to stay together Babe, see you at dinnertime.'

After I set up my bed, we have some downtime, so I run and sit on the beach. Cody comes over and sits with me.

'I think she still likes you,' I say teasingly.

'That girl won't take a hint.' He kicks at the sand like it's a football. 'do you now understand why I didn't want a girlfriend?'

'I can see why she likes you,' I tease him.

'Can you now?' he says, licking his lips again. 'Good!'

'It's the messy beach-swept hair. I bet she doesn't know you have a foot fetish. Handing out socks to strangers and stealing shoes,' I laugh.

He lets out a boom of a laugh. 'She most definitely doesn't know the real me. It's all an image for her. I have known her for three years, and I think you know me better already.'

'Possibly,' I say, giggling, 'but I look at the world differently. I better go.' Dumb bladder, rushing me away.

'See you at dinner.'

I run to the dorm, busting for a pee, and Nina's blocking the doorway.

'Sandra,' she says.

'Hi,' I wriggle.

'What were you talking to Cody about?'

'Oh, is that his name?' I say, 'We were talking about this girl Rebecca, who was here at trials, but she didn't make it.' Mum can always tell when I lie – I hope Nina can't. 'Rebecca was my friend, and she had a thing with his friend Rylie.'

'His name is Ryder, not Rylie. You are bad with names, aren't you? You talk to Cody a lot,' she says scowling.

'I talk to lots of people, and I don't always remember their names. Is that a problem?'

'No, not at all,' she says in a fake voice.

I add, 'I think that you just notice me talking to Cody more than others because you're always watching him.'

'That's because he's mine. He and I have something special.' She finally lets me pass so I can reach the bathroom.

The surf team is all given matching red and white clothes—togs, sweats, and tees, so I dress in them and chat with the other girls in the dorm.

Of us girls, Meg and Rose are sharing a room, as are Nina and I. Petra, Ariana, Dawn, and Alex each have a room of their own.

At our first meal, I talk to all the girls and get to know some guys, too. There are a lot more guys than gals. Cody looks so hot in his red singlet and shorts. He winks at me in my togs and board shorts.

After dinner, Nina plonks herself next to me. 'Soooo, Sandra. Tell me about you?'

'I like to surf.' I shift uncomfortably. Why can't I shake her off? Now I really know how Cody feels.

'What and who else do you like?'

'I love the Seagulls.' I name my favourite band.

'I mean boys.' Her smile cracks a little. She doesn't really think I am buying her charade, does she?

After fifteen minutes of being pressed for who my crush is, I say, 'The one with the curly hair is cute,' just to shut her up. Seeing half the guys have curly hair, I hope I've got away with it. You could even say Cody has a curl in his hair. It's more of a wave, though.

Good Things Take Time.

Finally, I have my first day at work. I'm in Cody's team, and although I don't get a moment alone with him, he gently touches my back or shoulders in passing a few times. Cody doesn't do that to anyone else. He's very serious and focused during our shifts. We take turns watching the surf from the tower and patrolling the sand. I am glad to have Petra in our group. Petra is not someone I would want to piss off, but she's a great person to have in your corner – and I hope she stays in mine.

By our second day, the six of us in our team go for a hilarious game of mini-golf.

At home, we have a makeshift mini-golf course. Ours is not quite as mini and doesn't have cute bridges and lighthouses like this one at the beach does, but I easily get a handful of hole-in-one's beating the others.

Cody walks over to me when I'm alone and whispers in amusement, 'Is there anything you can't beat me at?'

I refrain from replying, *making the first move.*

He slides his hand down my back, and for the first time, he touches my bottom before he walks away.

I look up and see Petra is watching us. I turn redder than my uniform.

Back at the beach, I go for a run alone. The calming rate I run falls into a natural rhythm, and the crashing of the waves make an unpredictable sound. They make me want to sing – that is – if I could hold a tune.

When I get back, the others are sitting around a bonfire. Nina is trying to cosy up to Cody, but his body language is leaning away from her. He glares at Ryder. Ryder shrugs.

Arriving late, everyone looks up at me.

Awkwardly, I crawl between Ryder and Petra.

'Hi,' I say.

'Don't be nasty, Nina,' Cody spits.

I blush, feeling like they have been talking about me.

'Hi Sandra, I just told the others who you think is cute,' Nina giggles.

'I didn't, I haven't...,' I glare at Nina, feeling my skin boil.

She laughs, 'Just kidding. I didn't say anything. Your secret is safe with me.'

Cody smiles at me and then turns to Nina and shakes his head.

Ryder and Cody pick up guitars, and we have a few sing-a-longs. I didn't want to be the first one to leave. But the minute Petra gets up for bed, I leave, too.

'You, okay?' Petra asks.

'Was she talking about me?' I ask.

'She's a bitch,' Petra avoids answering, so I know that's a yes.

'Tomorrow, come see me before the night's entertainment. I'll help you,'

The next day at work, I'm paired up with Cody. The fine weather is having a break, but it's not raining enough to close the beach.

During a break in the weather, Cody says, 'Let's go on rubbish duty.' So, we wander along in silence, picking up rubbish. He speaks first, 'Did you tell Nina that you liked me?'

I blush. 'No'

'So, what did you say?'

'She kept pushing me for who I liked for ages, so I said the guy with curly hair just to get her off my back and realised that a few of you have curly hair. I thought that would be the end of it.'

'Oh,' he says.

He has a cute, *thinking* look on his face.

'Is there a story?' I ask, tossing in an empty Fanta bottle.

'There are so many stories,' he says, collecting a pile of wrappers.

'This spot's awesome. Let's sit here for a second.' We sit between two large mounds of dark sand. 'It's so beautiful here.'

'You're so beautiful.' He touches my face.

I turn the colour of his red singlet, which shows off just how much he takes care of his body.

'You have real natural beauty. I literally haven't been able to take my eyes off you since the day we met,' he says.

I'm shocked.

'Trouble is, the day you arrived... Nina thought she was my girlfriend. And she has been watching me, watching you, and I think I have made you a target. I am sorry,' he says with an apologetic sigh.

'What do you mean by natural beauty?' I question.

'You see Nina, she's beautiful.' He looks from me to the shore.

'Yeah, she is.' I'm now feeling deflated.

'It takes two hours every morning for her to look like that. She has beauty appointments twice a week. How much time did you spend getting ready for work this morning?'

'Two minutes, four if you include brushing my teeth.'

He smiles. 'Nina can be a real cow. I think she is playing with you. That's why I wanted to warn you. I don't want her thinking you like me 'cause it will make it harder for you.'

'I never said that I do, just that you are cute. I have to know someone before I like them.'

'Ain't that the truth,' he says, lifting his eyebrows. 'If I had known Nina like I do now, I never would have looked at her twice.'

'How long did you date?'

'A few nights according to me, but two years according to her.'

'Two years. Wow! That makes sense as to why she's so upset.'

'I like the way you look more than her, your natural windswept look. How can I impress you?' he swivels to face me.

'Hey, I have already admitted I think you are cute,' I say.

'You're adorable when you blush like this. I want to get to know you better. Is that all right?' he hesitates.

'Yes, but what about Nina? She's my roommate.'

'Of course she is. She's playing games with you. She has seen me watching you. Has she asked you if you have a boyfriend?'

'No, she's only asked leading questions to see if I like you. Which I failed.'

He grabs my hand again, and it feels like I'm turning into jelly.

'How about you tell her you have a boyfriend?'

'I can't lie,' I say honestly.

'You are so adorable,' he says, moving closer to me. 'Let's say I'm your boyfriend.'

'Well, she won't like that.'

'No, but would you?'

Butterflies are having a dance party in my tummy.

'I think so,' I admit.

He moves closer again. My fingers reach out, hoping for a touch.

'I can tell you some things about me she doesn't know, and when you talk about me, your boyfriend, she will think it's someone else.'

I can't speak, so I just nod and grin.

'I can say the same. That will take the pressure off us, and then perhaps we can go on some dates and get to know each other better.'

'I would like that,' I squeak.

'I would like to kiss you.'

'Me? I've never kissed anyone before.' My face is as hot as the bonfire last night.

Now it's his turn to say, 'Really? Are there no guys where you come from? They should have been lining up around the block to kiss you.'

'I have four big brothers. No one is allowed near me,' I chuckle.

'Oh,' he says, moving further away.

'Don't go,' I say, grabbing his wrist and pulling him back. 'I like it when you are close

like this. You give me a funny feeling in my
tummy.'

'Me too,' he says, and for the first time, his
face is scarlet.

'Can we try something?' he runs his
thumb over mine. 'Let's see if I can move
those butterflies a little more.'

He puts one hand on my stomach and
moves his hand in circles.

I smile.

He moves closer and kisses me on the
cheek.

'How was that?' he asks.

I giggle.

He moves in again and kisses my lips
quickly. The pressure of his lips is more
breathtaking than I'd anticipated.

'Was that ok?'

I lay down on my back, breathing in the
fresh salt air, feeling like I could skip on
top of the ocean. 'That was the best feeling
ever. Can we do that again sometime?'

I've finally had his lips on mine. My first
kiss.

'Often, I hope,' he gently walks his fingers
up and down my arm. 'Things feel so
natural with you.'

He kisses me again, but for longer this time, and he is back to rubbing my thumb with his thumb. He tastes of salt, and I want more.

'Want to come surf with me after work? I know a more private place.'

'Yes, please.'

'You better tell me some of those secret things about you, then.'

'We better head back to work. I'll tell you as we go, but I think we should try one more kiss first.'

I nod, my face burning.

I'm still lying down, and he slowly eases down on top of me and kisses my cheek. Then he keeps kissing me across my face till he reaches my lips. This time, he moves his lips more, parting mine, and I feel his tongue.

My whole body comes alive, like an electric buzzing that ignites me. Our mouths keep moving together. It's the most amazing feeling, and I never want it to stop.

The walkie-talkie beeps, and we break apart.

'How's it looking up there, Cody? Is the beach clean? Over.' Petra's voice crackles.

'For the next three minutes till the families trash it again, over,' Cody replies.

He runs his hands down my face and bops my nose gently again.

I give him a goofy grin.

'Okay, head back. We'll swap.'

As we walk back, we talk. 'I love Pokémon. I collect and trade the cards,' he says, still rubbing his thumb on mine as we hold hands.

I try not to laugh as he tells me other goofy things he does. 'Oh my gosh, you're a nerd,' I tease him. 'This is why I need to get to know you. Nina will never know it's you when I tell her my boyfriend plays Pokémon,' I tease. 'Are you my boyfriend, or is it just a trick for Nina?'

He gets down on one knee. 'Sandra Welch, will you be my girlfriend, please?' He looks at me like he's melting into the steaming sand.

'Yes, please.' I focus on my poker face again so he doesn't know just how giddy he has me feeling. Boyfriend! Cody is my boyfriend! Mine.

We keep walking and talking. As we get closer, we let go of each other's hands.

'I manipulated many things to put you on this shift with me,' he tells me.

'Did you?' I ask.

'And every other shift,' he says, winking. 'And Nina is on the shift before or after us, so we get lots of time alone.'

'Bring it on,' I grin, still like a goof. 'My Pokénerd, who can ride a unicycle while dressed up as a clown. I am one lucky gal.'

The next day, I'm working the shoreline when I see a kid waving his hand in the air between dumps. I run and start calling to him. 'I'm coming. Listen to my voice. I'm Sandra, and I am on my way to help you.'

He calms down as I get closer until another wave crashes over him, causing his panic levels to rise again.

I dive under the wave and swim up beside him. 'What's your name?'

'I'm going to die!' he is trying to move forward but going out deeper.

'No,' I say. 'We are not that deep.' I stand and reach out for him. 'Another wave is coming. Hold your nose after a breath, follow me, dive under the wave. I won't let go of you.'

Thankfully, he does as I ask, and as soon as the wave has passed, I start paddling him ashore. We're halfway in when Cody reaches us.

There's a group of people at the shore watching now, including a lady in tears. His mum, I guess.

Cody tries to take the boy off me, but the boy clings on tight.

'Ethan.' The crying lady calls as we arrive back to dry land. 'Are you okay?'

'Thank you. What's your name?' The boy's father puts his arms on his son's shoulders.

The boy is still gripping me.

'My name's Sandra.' I try to step away so his parents can hold him, but he follows me. 'Water is fun but strong and dangerous. Have you learned anything today, Ethan?'

'I learnt you are my angel. I think I love you.'

I wish I couldn't see Cody in my peripheral vision. He's holding back a laugh, and I need to stay staunch.

Afterwards, I have lots of paperwork to fill out, and Cody helps me. When he's stopped laughing, that is. This is why I'm here, to make a difference. I don't need Cody giving me special feelings inside. I have them from my own actions. But Cody's praises help.

The next day, the little boy, Ethan, brings me a bunch of flowers and a strawberry sponge cake, which I share with everyone. For the rest of the week, Ethan gives me flowers every day. By the looks of it ones he's picked on his way to the beach.

I get into the swing of things – finally used to wearing the belt over my shoulders with the radio in it. The daily health and safety paperwork becomes second nature, and the weather game is always fun. Every morning, we check the surf report and weather report. And then I give my prediction. By the second week, my predictions have all been correct, and the others come to me for reports instead of their phones – city kids know nothing. Knowing the weather for the waves is just as important as knowing it for farming.

A week later, I'm walking past Ethan, and I say, 'Hi Ethan, how are you today?'

'Good, Sandra.' He walks up beside me.

Cody is next to me, but Ethan never acknowledges Cody or any of the other lifesavers.

'Sandra, why didn't you give me mouth to mouth because I want your mouth on mine?' Cheeky little Ethan puts his arms around me and tries to kiss me. My hand makes it in front of my mouth just in time.

I turn to face Ethan. 'The first thing you need to know is that you never just put your mouth on someone else's without asking. My boyfriend spent weeks leading up to the first time he kissed me, and his lips are the only lips that go on mine.'

Ethan takes a step away from me, puts both his hands on his heart, and falls back into the black sand.

'Save me, Sandra, my heart's breaking. Save me by being mine.'

His mum scoffs, 'Ethan!'

Cody can't contain his laughter anymore. He and I run off to the tower.

'Well handled,' he says, giving me a secretive kiss in the tower, which he doesn't normally do.

Cody then tells the others what they have missed so they can all laugh at me while I sort out the paperwork.

Getting Old

After my shift, I float to the carpark. Excited about our planned escape. Cody is already by his car. He walks over and helps me with my surfboard, putting it on his roof rack with his board. His warm hand slips into mine, and he walks me to his passenger door, opening it for me.

I sit, putting my bag at my feet. I have to do up my seat belt to stop from floating away.

Cody jumps into the driver's side; it's cleaner than I thought a boy's car would be. Cleaner than any of my brothers' cars, that's for sure.

We drive to a new beach I haven't been to before and as soon as the boards are off the roof we run over the burning black sand into the waves and surf. This time, when we finish surfing, we put our boards down on the sand. Cody picks me up and walks me back into the waves, where we make out.

'Every single time I have seen you in the waves, I have wanted to do this,' he says, kissing me some more.

We spend a little longer at the beach, making out first in the waves and then on the sand.

'I'm making the most of this. Sorry, I can't kiss you this much at work,' he murmurs against my lips.

'I don't mind.'

We walk back to the car, still holding hands and sharing the odd kiss.

'Who's keeping secrets, Cody?'

We turn and see Tyson, a lifeguard from a different group, standing there. He has his arms around a short, dark, and handsome guy.

'Hey,' I say as Cody takes a step away from me.

'I'll keep your secret if you keep mine,' Tyson says as he kisses the guy he's holding.

'Are you still in the closet?' His boyfriend laughs at him.

'Shush you.' He kisses him quietly while Cody and I laugh.

'Sure. Hi, I'm Cody, and this is my girlfriend, Sandra.' Cody shakes hands with Tyson's boyfriend. He steps back towards me and drapes his arm around my shoulder.

'Hi, I'm Lee.'

We carry on to the car, and once the boards are loaded up, we head back.

'Wow,' I say from one side of the car as we tie the boards on the roof.

'I know – imagine if it'd been someone else.'

'Like Nina,' I say grimly, putting my gear in the boot.

'Don't ruin a good day out by saying her name.'

'Sorry,' I say as we both take our seats. Cody starts the car.

'I'm glad he knows at least we have someone to watch our back.'

'Suppose.' Cody turns the music on. I guess he's still not ready to admit he's with me to the world. The music was welcome since our outing was ruined – even without Nina. Or was it still because of her?

That night, we all sit around outside again.

Cody and Ryder weren't there when I got there, so I sit next to Tyson.

Cody and Ryder finally come out to join us. Ryder sits next to me and Cody, opposite from Nina.

Sadly, the minute Cody looks comfortable, Nina crawls over to sit behind Cody, and she massages his shoulders and neck.

Cody looks at Ryder, his eyes and lips telling Ryder a story—telling Ryder to sort his sister out.

'Enough, Nina, please go back and sit down,' Cody snaps after Ryder says nothing.

Cody, still looking at Ryder, holds his hands and starts counting Five, four, three...

Ryder stands up. 'Nina, please come for a walk with me.'

'Later,' she says, wrapping her arms around Cody and laying her head on his shoulder.

At that moment, Tyson puts his arm around me. I lean in, appreciating Tyson's support.

'Now!' Ryder demands.

'I'll be back, babe.' Nina kisses Cody on his cheek and skips off after Ryder.

When they are far enough away, Cody says, 'Hey guys, Nina is beautiful. Will one of you date her, please? Please!'

A few of them laugh.

'Please,' he begs. 'I have an amazing new girlfriend. Imagine if she sees the way Nina keeps falling all over me. Any of you, please.'

'Are you crazy? We have all seen how nuts she has been at you for two years! Why would we want that?' Api laughs.

'She's not that bad,' her best friend defends her.

'I didn't say she was. Only that we were over years ago, and she won't take the hint. I have someone else, and Nina is still trying it on. I don't know what to do.'

'Cody, bring your girlfriend here. She'll take the hint,' Meg says.

'I will in a few weeks,' Cody looks directly at me. Petra does, too.

Nina returns and goes right back to grabbing at Cody.

He turns and says something to her, stands up, and storms off.

I want to follow him, but that will be too obvious. Ryder runs after him anyway.

'He broke up with you. Leave him be,' Petra hisses.

'We're only on a break,' Nina snaps.

'Well, leave him alone then. Now, we can't have our sing-along just because you are getting on his nerves.'

Petra and Meg get up and leave. A few others, too.

'He still likes me.' I hear Nina say to her friend Ariana.

'It may be time to move on,' Ariana says back to her.

'Come for a walk with me, Sandra,' Tyson says, reaching his hand out for me.

'Off to the dunes, you two,' someone says behind us.

Tyson puts one arm around me and drops it to my bottom.

'Sorry,' he whispers.

'So much drama,' I say. We walk along the beach and see Cody and Ryder running towards us.

Cody must want to run his frustrations off.

'So, you two are a couple now? Interesting,' Ryder says, looking over at

Cody before he runs past us and back to the bonfire.

'I'll catch up soon.' Cody bends down to do his shoelace.

'Get your hands off my girl,' Cody says between his teeth when Ryder has gone.

'You know she's not my type, but I have to say, it looks like someone else is your girl. Don't break Sandra's heart.' Tyson stomps away, leaving us alone.

I keep walking away from the clubhouse, and Cody comes up beside me. 'I'm sorry.'

'I know. It's getting old though, isn't it?'

'So old!'

Cody slips his hand in mine. 'You are the only person I kiss. I promise.'

'Prove it.' I reject his hand and run off.

He chases me, and eventually, I let him catch me, pulling me down to the sand with him and rolling on top. Grinning, he pins me down and kisses me the hardest he has yet.

The next hour is fantastic.

News is Spreading

There are six lifeguards on a shift—four girls and two guys. One of the girls, Petra, is dating the other senior, Api. I suspect that the other two girls, Meg and Rose, are secretively a couple too. They are roommates in the dorm. It means that everyone on our shift has eyes for each other, so hopefully, they won't notice that Cody and I are into each other. But one girl does.

'Sandra, come for a walk with me,' Petra says the next morning before our shift.

Doesn't help that my boyfriend has a protective watch over me already, and he stands as Petra pulls me away. Cody pretends to look in a different direction.

As soon as we have walked out of earshot, Petra spoke, 'Girl, you're stepping in some big shoes.'

'What do you mean?'

'Nina wants her man back and will throw you under a bus to get him.'

'I don't know what you mean,' I try to say calmly.

'Cody has had his eye attached to you even more so than normal the last few days. We all see it, and you are the same with him. I guess you guys finally got together after flirting for over a month.'

'How do you know?' My eyes bulge – Cody doesn't want anyone to know. I hope he doesn't get mad at me. 'Please don't say anything.'

'It's so obvious to us in this group. But I guess that's why Cody put us all in this group because we're not the kind of people to go and talk to Nina. You have to watch your back. She's vicious. I suggest you try to change rooms if you get the chance. The way you and Cody look at each other – everyone's gonna know soon enough, and that's not gonna be good for your little sleeping situation.'

'Oh,' I say.

'I'll help you when we get back. Or are you heading out with Cody after this?' she winks.

'Yes,' I grin.

'Just tell him to give you fifteen minutes first. We'll come up with a plan. I've known Cody for three years and have never seen him like he is with you. You guys must have something special.'

I grin some more.

When we get back, Cody comes to see me the first chance he subtly can. 'What did she say?'

'To watch out for Nina and that they all know about us.' I look away, hoping he will finally tell Nina about me.

'Petra!' he yells, kicking the sand.

'Yeah,' she says, walking towards us, grinning.

'Who knows?' he demands.

'Just the six of us,' she says, 'and I assume Tyson after he walked off with her at the bonfire.'

'Yip, he knows,' I say, pressing my lips together.

'Cody, you follow her like a puppy,' she teases him.

'So how can we keep it secret?' he does look like a puppy dog begging.

'Telling us is a start. We can have Sandra's back.'

'Thanks Petra.' Cody's shoulders relaxed. 'I really like Sandy.'

'Sandy?' my eyes narrow. Is that a pet name or a *not-my-girlfriend* name?

'You are my Sandy,' Cody gives me a quick kiss but keeps his arms around my waist.

'None of us like Nina,' Petra says. 'She is plotting to get you back. She tells everyone you are still together, just secretly.'

The rest of the afternoon, Cody tells the others about our relationship and how we need more opportunities to be together. We talk a lot about it. Too much – I'm not used to being the person with the drama. I prefer the shadows.

Petra confirms she is dating Api. She says that I can share her room and we will tell the others it's because we're in the same crew. That makes sense.

We make a plan. Api and Cody go surfing after work while Petra and I move my stuff into her room. That night, Cody will talk of meeting a fake girlfriend.

I text James and ask him to call me, pretending to be my boyfriend.

Cody doesn't talk about his 'girlfriend' in front of Nina, but she overhears his conversations.

Our plan goes smoothly, and more importantly, it works! Nina treats me like a no-one again. She's walking around, acting sad all the time. After one fake call, Nina asks, 'Who's your boyfriend?' in a monotone voice.

'He's so cute,' I smile.

'I used to have a cute boyfriend,' she stalks away. She must like him, but there is so much she doesn't even know about him. She only likes the idea of Cody.

James

The next time I see Nina perk up is on the weekend when a tall, lean, red-headed guy arrives at the surf club.

I run up to him and jump into his arms.

Arm in arm, we walk off chatting as everyone looks on from the club – especially Cody and Nina.

I'm so glad to see James. He raises his eyebrows, 'So, what's this trouble you are in?'

'There's no trouble,' I say. 'Just everyone has boyfriends, and it's a bit of a big deal here. I didn't want the drama, so I faked one. Hope you don't mind?'

I squint past the sun, up at the people watching from the clubhouse. 'Come up, I'll introduce you to some friends. My shift starts soon. Do not let that blonde with the perfect smile and the legs up to her armpits near you,' I say.

I bulge my eyes at him, and he laughs at me, trying to brush it off as a joke. 'I'm serious. There's a Barbie doll type here who thinks she's God's gift to men.'

'No matter how pretty she is, she'll never distract me from my number one gal.' James already has his perfect girl back home. I adore her and already treat her like my sister.

He opens a ring box with an engagement ring to show me.

There are all sorts of ohhhhs and noises from up above. They think he's asking me to marry him. He puts the ring away, and I hug him.

'When are you asking her?'

'I don't know. What do you think?'

'Sandy, we gotta set up,' Cody calls.

It's the first time he's called me Sandy in front of the others. Why is he calling me when we still have ten minutes up our sleeves? Surely, he's not feeling threatened.

I grab James's hand. 'Come,' I say, running up the stairs.

I walk to Petra first. 'Petra, this is my brother. He wants advice on how to ask his girl to marry him. Can he come with us to set up?'

'He sure can,' Cody answers, looking a lot more relaxed again. 'But only if you tell us all Sandra's secrets.'

Thirty minutes later, we sit around our patch, all set up for the day, talking romantic proposal ideas.

'A plane with a banner. Will you marry me?' Api says.

'No,' say all the girls together.

'Not in food or drink, where the girl dies choking on the ring either,' Cody says.

We all laugh.

'She likes bush walks. Just take her on a walk somewhere special. You could always talk to Dad about which part of the farm he is going to give you to build on. That would be a brilliant spot.'

'It would be,' everyone agrees.

Nina comes up and joins us.

'What's going on here?' she asks, looking my brother up and down.

'Sandra's brother is about to ask his girlfriend to marry him,' Rose says.

'Oh,' Nina says. 'Put the ring in a glass of Champagne.'

'Nice one,' Cody says with a straight face. We all hide our laughter.

Out in the surf, some kids are near a rip. 'I'm going out,' I say.

'I'll go too.' Cody and Petra both want to get away from Nina.

We head out and move a group of boys away from the rip. Safe and secure.

Nina leaves the tower, too, and is up in the dunes watching Cody.

I run ahead of Cody and Petra and pretend to call my boyfriend.

When I turn back, Nina has gone, and the others have caught up to me.

I tell Cody, 'Nina's been watching you.'

'Stalker,' Petra hisses.

As we head up the stairs, there's a spot where no one can see us. Cody knows it, because he kisses me in that spot more passionately than he ever has.

'You know I like you?' I nudge him.

'I was jealous. Silly ah,' he says.

But at that moment, we look up and see James looking down at us. Open-mouthed staring.

He's seen us kiss. I thought he'd be mad, but he winks. We climb up as James laughs. 'I need to go, sis, but first, I want to get to know Cody a little better.' Cody reaches out for a handshake.

'We hug in our family, mate,' James brings Cody in for a group hug. 'Can you come for a walk, Cody?' James asks, and the two of them head off.

I watch the waves and keep an eye on my two favourite guys. They're laughing and seem to get along well. Hopefully, James doesn't come down too heavy. He's never had this chance before. I dread what he will go home and tell the rest if the family.

Finally, they come back over. 'Bring him up to the farm soon, sis,' he says. 'You've got my support when you choose to tell Dad.' He hugs us both and leaves. My shoulders are lighter, and my heart is fuller. I hadn't realised how much I needed that little visit from home.

That night, everyone from the surf club has another bonfire. A couple drinks thrown into the mix, and we end up playing a game. Everyone takes turns asking a question, and then we answer it in a circle. They're all simple questions. Your favourite food, drink, book, movie, if you could holiday anywhere in the world, where would you go? – that is – until Nina's turn. 'Where did you lose your virginity?'

Of course, I haven't. This isn't something I want to talk about, and I don't want to hear any stories about Cody. I'm very relieved when Cody jumps up and says, 'It's dark. Let's swim.'

My concerns ease quickly, but that's when I realise by swim, he means swim naked. So those concerns come back and double. Another thing I have never done before. No one else seems self-conscious, and they're all in the water before I have taken my top off. I can't see their bits, and I am sure grateful it's not a full moon. Hopefully, they can't see me. A slow breath in and an exhale. I take my underwear off and charge into the waves. It's such a weird feeling having the waves up against my body, my skin red from embarrassment – not sunburn.

Cody laughs at me, probably 'cause I'm feeling shy. The funny thing is, it's so dark no one can see anything unless they are right next to me. Naturally, Cody is the closest to me. We move away from the others and hug. I can't believe I'm naked, and Cody is naked, and we are holding each other. We kiss in the dark, and he runs his hands over my back as I do his. He will be able to feel my breasts against his chest, and I can feel a part of him I'm not sure I'm ready to feel yet. Regardless, I'm intrigued. I can hear people getting closer.

'Cold enough for you, Nina,' Petra calls, warning us.

I swim away from Cody under the waves and paddle back towards the shore.

As I put my warm clothes back on, I hear Nina say, 'We need to be together. This body is all yours.'

'Solid pass. I have someone else now.'

'Who?'

'A girl from a few bays away.'

'You should be with me. It will be better than last time, I promise.'

'I don't like the way you treat other people,' Cody says bluntly.

'Babe, we belong together,' she tries again.

'No, Nina, we are never getting back together. Please leave me alone.' I hear him coming out of the water, too.

Nina runs in front of him and passes me. She grabs her gear and leaves.

Cody is dressed again by the time he catches up to me, sliding his hand in mine.

'I am heading back. It's been a big day.'

'Me too,' he says. 'I like you, and I'm so glad we are together. They're set for a long night of drinking. We're on the early shift, so it's probably a good thing we head to bed now. Want to meet at six for a run?'

'That sounds amazing.' I pull him in for another kiss –thank you darkness. We head off to separate beds.

I quietly sneak into the dorm rooms and can hear Nina sobbing. She's a cow, but I didn't know she could cry like this. I genuinely feel bad for her.

Nina yells, 'Answer your phone, Cody!'

I wake a few times by her yelling, and, at some stage, I hear a crash, followed by more tears.

Glad she doesn't know I'm inside and that I can hear her through the walls or that I'm the one with Cody now.

I fall asleep, dreaming of our run in the morning, hoping for more of those stolen kisses I love so much.

Home

The next morning, I wake up early.

I have time for yoga on the beach before Cody arrives.

'I could just watch you all day,' he laughs. 'Not in a stalker-ish way, although, I felt like one the first few days here.'

I can't help but think about Nina. I think they only saw each other at the beach for three years. That's why it's so hard on her now. The month they were first broken up, she wasn't here, seeing him. I guess it wouldn't have felt like they broke up in her mind. She's wanted to get him back, but now he says he has someone else. It's finally sinking in that she's lost him. I never want to lose him. 'Nina is pretty cut up about you guys,' I say.

'Yeah, she kept calling me last night.' He kicks at the sand.

'I heard.'

'She stopped about two in the morning.' He reaches a hand out for me, and I stand from my downward dog pose.

'I think that's because she threw and broke her phone,' I tell him.

'Oh. I realised we haven't given each other our numbers,' he says.

'No, I thought that too. But there's no need when we are here, is there?'

'No,' he agrees, 'let's run.'

'Although,' I say, jogging the familiar morning route, 'I am going home the next three days during our time off, so maybe we could have a text here or there when I'm away.'

'Maybe I could head your way for lunch one day,' he says.

'I would love that, but it's a two-hour drive.' We reach the end of the beach and turn up the alleyway to the road.

'That won't put me off,' he winks.

'We have an amazing beach close by.'

'How about I come for the day?' We loop back to the beach, over the dunes.

'Sounds great.'

We finish our run, set up for our shift, and just chill in the hut till the others slowly trail in. I'm curling his hair between my fingers, and he's just looking at me.

Today turns out to be a busy one. Too many saves and close calls and an ugly rip that catches three teenage guys, who have been rude till we save them. I guess they've learnt their lesson. Or at least got a shock and learnt to appreciate the power of the ocean. Ethan is still fully crushing on me and is constantly trying to get my attention. 'Sandra look... Sandra here... please Sandra....'

Everyone has a good laugh at him – he can't be older than twelve.

The others all go surfing after our shift. I head back to pack and pass Nina on the way.

She is still watching Cody. He looks up at me, and Nina sees him.

'What is it with you two?' she scoffs at me.

'Who two?' I ask her, focusing on my poker face.

'Cody,' she spits, her pretty face twitching.

'He's a great mentor,' I say. 'Like a big brother,' I add. 'I've got to go. I am heading home to see my man during my break. I can't wait.'

'Okay, have fun,' she says, happier.

Hopefully, I have side-tracked her.

I'm halfway home when I remember I've not given Cody my number, and no one else has it. I have it written on a piece of paper in my pocket, but each time I'd tried to hand it over, Cody had a fan club around him. I guess he won't be coming to see me. Oh man, I really wanted to show him around. It will be weird not running with him tomorrow morning.

At home, I get back to my normal swing of life, have a long ride on my horse, hang with my brothers, and help Mum pre-make some meals for the busy days when she's working with Dad and doesn't have time to cook.

Two of my brothers have been away at summer school, but they're driving back soon. There's always lots of work to be done, but we are all home this weekend.

Dad inherited the rest of the farm when Nana and Pops passed away. Us kids will always have a business and roof over our heads, but that means that there's always lots of work to do. He's leased a few of the paddocks out, but we still have fences to maintain, cattle to move, sheep to shear.

The second morning, I head into town at about ten. I go to the local food store, and Enita, who works there, calls out to me, 'Sandra, there was this hot guy in here asking for you.'

'Cody?' I ask.

I grab my stuff and run off, looking for him. I search for twenty minutes around the town.

My phone rings, and it's my brother, Chris. In his biggest teasing voice, he says, 'Sandra's got a boyfriend, Sandra's got a boyfriend! A young caller showed up at our door. He is currently being interrogated by Mum and Dad. Better come quick.'

it's the quickest I've ever driven home. All our cars are in the driveway next to Cody's. Hopefully, my brothers are helping – not hindering. I sprint up the verandah steps and crash open the front door. Dad and Cody are sitting at the table. Mum has wasted no time at all and has scones in the oven and the jug boiling.

I've never bought a guy home before. I've never had the opportunity. I hope my family hasn't scared him off. I've always been Daddy's little girl, so my legs are shaking and my face is about the same colour as Mum's homemade strawberry jam. I can imagine it's not what Cody is expecting, that's for sure.

I walk in, apologising, 'Cody, I never gave you my phone number.'

Dad stands up. 'You mean you know this boy, but you didn't invite him around?' Dad's face is now redder than the strawberry jam.

'No, no, no, Dad, this is Cody. Cody's my boyfriend.'

Mum strolls in, carrying the tray I could smell earlier. 'Is that meant to make it better, Sandra, dear?'

'No, no, no, Cody is my supervisor at work,' I try to recover, 'I mean–'.

'Sounds like he's doing a bit more than supervising you,' one of my brothers says from around the corner, followed by more laughter. Not helping.

My brothers are adults, and they still stand around the corner, eavesdropping on my conversations. Nice. I want to run into Cody's arms but have to play it cool. So I wink at him dorkily instead. He smiles back.

'I'd planned to meet Cody at the beach and show him the best surfing spots, but we forgot to exchange phone numbers. We haven't needed to call each other because we've been working together at the same place each day.' I'm getting tongue-tied. I take a big breath and try again. 'Cody is kind. I'm glad you guys are being so open-minded and getting to know him.'

There's more laughter from around the corner.

'Why don't you guys just come out?' I hiss at them.

James, Chris, Tony, and Richard all appear from around the corner and shake hands with Cody, well, except James. James hugs him.

Cody starts, 'I thought you hug in this house...what's with all the handshaking?'

Everyone turns to James.

'You mean you knew about Cody?' Dad grumps.

It's my turn to giggle.

It takes about an hour for everyone to have their conversations and eat scones. Then, finally, Cody and I head out to the beach.

When we are alone, Cody is laughing so much I can't even get out of him what's so hilarious? When he finally stops laughing, he gets his words out. 'So that's your family? I can see why you haven't had too many guys brave enough to come over.'

I relax and laugh, too.

'I have to tell you; I got the evils just asking some people in town about you. Until I asked Richard, who didn't tell me he was your brother – he just said to follow him, and he'd show me how to find the Welch Farm. Looking back on it, I guess I should've known. You don't normally just take a stranger to someone else's house, do you? I guess he knew where all the guns in the house would be.'

Within an hour, there are fifteen people at our private beach, half of us surfing. My brothers, their girlfriends, my dad and my uncle. My cousin Melissa, even has her new boyfriend come. I look to the shore and see

Mum arriving with her picnic bag. She and my aunty are setting food out.

I paddle over to Cody. 'Literally every member of my family is here at the beach.'

He laughs, distracted he gets dumped by the next wave.

We surf for a while and then see everyone going in for lunch. 'I'm sorry about my family,' I say.

'I want to hug you, but I am honestly scared a target will appear on my body, and your dad and brothers will all take aim.'

I laugh again. 'You forgot my uncle.'

'It will be even worse if I kiss you, right?' he asks.

I nod.

We're so used to hiding our relationship with everyone at the surf club that we don't need to hold each other now to prove we're an item, which I hope my parents' respect.

'Next time we go away,' I say, 'I want to go somewhere we can be alone all weekend long. I can't wait to kiss you again.'

'That sounds perfect,' he says. 'We have more time off together in a couple of weeks.'

'Yes,' I say, 'let's make a plan.'

We sit down, and I introduce Cody to the rest of the family. They all tell stories to share, designed to make my face strawberry jam coloured again. Cody just laughs. He seems relaxed around them. He genuinely fits in, which is such a relief.

That said, it still surprises me when my brothers ask Cody to stay the night and go to the stock cars with us.

Cody has to share a room with James, of course, and Vanessa, James's girlfriend (for now), comes too. As always, she stays in my room with me.

At the stock cars, everyone knows us, and we know everyone, but none of the locals pick up on the fact that the visitor is my boyfriend. I've finished my last year of school, and weirdly, no one thinks of me as at dating age. As the night rolls on, Zach comes up and tries to make a move on me. Andrew does, too. At this, Cody slides his hand down my back, subtly connecting us.

'Are you together?' Andrew asks.

'Absolutely,' I slide my arm around Cody's.

'Seriously?' Zach storms off.

'Does that mean we get to ask her out now?' Andrew asks one of my brothers.

'No,' Cody says, 'she's taken.'

At this point, he starts holding my hand, clearly marking his territory, and he doesn't relax his grip until he gently kisses me goodnight outside my bedroom door.

More dramas

The next morning, I get up early and take my horse for a ride.

When I come back, Cody's helping Mum collect eggs for breakfast.

After breakfast, everyone spends the rest of the morning helping Dad do jobs around the place.

James and Vanessa go to check the fences around the farm. James winks at me as he leaves, and Cody crosses his fingers before he heads off with Dad and Tony to do something with the cattle.

I slip back to the horses and clean the stables. Once they are clean, I head back inside to find Mum in the kitchen shelling peas. 'I'm just gonna bake a cake?' I take out the flour.

'Okay,' she says.

I bake a chocolate cake and while it cooks, I fill the fridge with drinks.

'What are you up to?' Mum laughs, watching me.

'You never know when you may have guests,' I say mysteriously.

'What do you know?' she asks.

'Nothing for sure, but I just have a feeling,' I say without giving anything away.

Three hours later, Mum's in a right pickle.

Cody was meant to head back to work, but everyone insists he stays for the celebration dinner.

Vanessa, her parents, and her brother are coming over for an engagement meal.

Leaning against the counter, Cody watches me with a gooey look on his face, as I mix shades of green icing, Vanessa and James's favourite colour, and apply it to the now cooled cake.

'I have never felt so at ease at someone else's house,' he says, dipping his finger into the icing bowl. I swat it away, but not before he has a taste and grins. 'I've known you for two months, dating for just over two weeks. Yesterday, I met all of your family, and today, I feel like they're my family, too.' He leans over and gives me a quick kiss.

'We like you too,' James says, walking in. 'That cake looks amazing, thanks.' James picks me up and spins me around. 'I'm getting married! Do you want to make our wedding cake?'

'Sure,' I say. 'Shall I start on it next weekend?'

'Maybe,' he says, 'I can't wait. Dad told me we will have a working bee on the Baxter house soon, and that will be our wedding gift from them.'

'Oh, James, I am so happy for you both. That's always been your pick of the houses.'

'Wait, what? You get a house as a wedding gift?' Cody asks.

I explain about the shared property.

'That's cool,' he says. 'How many houses are there?'

'Two others,' I say. 'I can show you later if you like. One is run down, and the other is rented.'

'Sounds great.'

After lunch the next day, Cody and I drive back in his car as we will both come back together for the working bee next weekend.

Music is pumping in his car. We take turns choosing songs and finding out what music we have in common, then teasing each other about what we don't.

We finally exchange phone numbers, and as we arrive back at the beach, it's late, so we say goodnight, and I crawl into bed without seeing or talking to anyone.

The next morning, I still rise early and take off on my run. I run into Cody, and we jog the rest of the circuit together before jumping into the ocean for a swim.

Refreshed from the dip in the ocean, I head back to the dorm to have a shower. I'm floating on air, feeling adored and in love. That quickly changes.

By the time I head back to the beach, I see Nina slapping Cody and yelling at him outside the clubhouse. 'Lier, Cheat, Bastard.' I want to run between them to protect him. I am about to when she turns around and storms past me, grabbing her things, as she is still screaming at him. Everyone has their heads poked around a corner, or looking over their coffee mugs, watching the drama unfold.

Nina's brother goes to see what's going on. After a brief chat with Nina, he runs over to Cody. Cody ducks as if Ryder is going to hit him. But he doesn't.

Part of me wants to hear what's going on; part of me wants to hide and never find out.

They talk, and then Ryder drives his sister down the road.

'Did you hear?' Petra says as she brushes her teeth.

'Not really. Just yelled words.' I admit not wanting to know.

'Nina said that Cody cheated on her, and she has quit work!' Petra spat out.

'Honestly?' I spit out toothpaste and tie my hair back.

'He just stood there and said nothing, didn't defend himself or anything.' Meg washed her face.

'No, he did – he leaned in close and whispered something that turned her face whiter than a ghost.

'What?' Meg and I ask.

'No idea. But it must have been something as that's when she stormed off.'

'It's going to be quiet around here.' Petra takes my hair tie out of my hair and puts it up nicer.

'It's going to be peaceful.' Meg laughs.

On the way to the tower, I sidetrack and run over to Cody to get him alone. 'You okay?'

'She was on at me about dating her. I couldn't handle it, so I told her how I spent the weekend at my girlfriend's place and how serious I am with her – with you.' He looks from the sand to me. 'Nina realised how she had made a fool out of herself, and she just left. Screaming insults.'

'The screaming I heard.'

Petra's right. The next few days are relaxing. A lot of the girls become more chilled talking to the boys, including my Cody.

They've all feared Nina, or at the very least, were intimidated by her. Me too, I guess.

After the shower, we are called into the club house for a meeting.

'Time to choose a name out of a hat for a five-dollar Secret Santa gift.

I pull out Ryder's name. That will be challenging as I don't know anything about him except he has a crazy sister, a string of lovers, and an amazing best friend. At least I don't have his sister.

At the bonfire on Wednesday night, Cody pulls me away from the others. 'I want to give you a little more Nina background if that's okay. I don't want you to hear the wrong story.'

'Okay.' I slip my hand in his as we walk towards the golden sunset.

'You know how I asked you to be my girlfriend? Well, I never did that with Nina. The first year, I just thought it was a fling, and after summer, I went back home – never saw or talked to her. If I hadn't been too busy studying, I might have had other girlfriends too. When we came back for the weekend retreat, she was acting like we were a couple again.' He holds my hand as we walk down the beach. 'I told her it had just been a fling. The second night, when I was drunk, she came on to me real hard and sorry, but we ended up sleeping together. But it was just once.'

My stomach jerks. I guessed he had experience... I just hoped it wasn't with her.

'When I saw her again, she told me she was pregnant, so I had to do the right thing and support her. The next thing I knew, she had lost the baby and was upset, so I stayed by her side for the summer, but we never kissed or anything. I held her when she needed me to. I played Mr. Nice because I felt so bad for her. I thought I was supporting her as a friend. Over winter, we went our own ways again. The next time I saw her, I'd met you, and you were, and still are, all I think about — the only person I want to be with.' He gives me a quick kiss before continuing, 'Sorry you have had to hear all this, but I would rather you heard it from me.'

'Wow,' I say, 'that's a lot for you both to go through. Are you ok?' They lost a child together. No wonder they have a connection. And they had sex. I don't mean to but pull away from him.

'No, please come back, Sandy.' He reaches out for me.

'I am here for you.' I pull him down on the sand with me and kiss him. I need him to know I appreciate him telling me this, even if I don't like it.

We hear laughing and a wolf whistle and look up at a couple of lifeguards I don't really know looking at us.

'Please don't say anything yet,' Cody calls.

They laugh and keep walking.

'Nina is gone now. We'll wait a few days and come out in the open about us. I want to hold you all the time. I can't wait to go back to your farm, that is, if you still want me to.'

'Of course I do. I want to take you horse riding next time,' I add.

'I'd love that,' he says.

We have our special spot at the beach where people can't see us, and I think we've done enough talking, so we just lie there kissing for a while till I start shivering from the cold instead of his touch.

Birthday

Today I've turned seventeen, and as far as I'm aware... nobody here knows! I'm hoping to keep it that way. Because, ugh... birthdays are so embarrassing. All eyes on me? No thank you!

Cody cuts our morning run short. Bugger, I wanted some more time alone with him today, but it's not as if he knows.

We have the early shift, so I don't think we will have any time to make out, but to compensate, Cody shortens our run by five minutes each way, so we still have ten minutes in the dunes.

Even though we've had our run and kissing sesh, Cody and I are still the first ones at work. We get busy setting up for the day and end up on different jobs. The heat is scorching already, so we know it will be a busy one.

Halfway through the shift, I see Cody talking to a rowdy group of teenagers and adults alike. As I look closer at the group, I feel like crawling under the closest stone and hiding.

My whole family is there — cousins and uncle, and even my brothers' girlfriends. By the looks of the area they had commandeered, they've been here for a while.

I've been out in the surf with Petra. We'd told a few groups off for littering and done a rubbish run as well as manning the area between the flags, and they'd been there watching me the whole time.

I wave at them, and they wave back, and then most of them run out in the waves as I climb back to the tower.

'Do you know them?' Petra asks.

'Yes. That's my whole family,' I admit.

'You should go see them,' Petra grins.

'No, I'm working. We finish our shift in an hour. They will be more impressed that I carry on working. Looks like I'll get to spend the afternoon with them.'

'Petra, can I see you, please?' Cody says, coming up to us.

He gives my hand a squeeze before the two of them walk off.

After my shift, dressed casually, I run down to my family. Cody, Petra and Api join us. I introduce them all and spend the afternoon fooling around playing rugby, swimming, and having a ball.

Mum pulls out a cake.

'Please, Mum, I don't want everyone knowing.'

'It was on your registration information; you think we don't know? It's on the notice board in the club.' Cody laughs, 'Happy birthday! By the way, I have something sorted for later.'

It is a really fun afternoon, and several other lifesavers walk over to us. I introduce my family to them before they carry on doing their own thing, eating the cake that Mum insists I hand around, even though they're on duty.

My family leaves late afternoon, and I go in to have a shower. When I come back out, there's an envelope on my bed, like a little clue.

*Go to the place where we had
our first kiss.*

I call for Petra, and she helps put
makeup on to match a new pink dress
Mum has given me as a birthday gift.
Petra's been teaching me about makeup,
and I can apply some of it, but I prefer she
still helps while she can.

I walk out to the dunes where Cody and I
had our first kiss. When I get there, there's
a big heart channelled into the sand, and
the inside of the channel is filled with
flower petals. In the middle, under a rock,
is another envelope. I open it.

Go to the place where you earned the
bracelet *tied around your wrist.*

I run up to the clubhouse and to the
darts board. Another envelope inside with
a pair of scissors and a note saying Your
bracelet *is worn out. Now, it's time for*
a replacement.

Reluctantly, I cut the bracelet off. The
next note says in blue calligraphy Go
to the place where we are the most
serious.

We are both serious when we're at work, so I walk over to the tower. As I climb, I notice with a gasp that it's filled with lit candles.

Cody is sitting at a table with no less than thirty candles surrounding him on every surface available. There are even more rose petals on the table.

Cody looks up at me. 'Happy birthday, beautiful.' He stands up, I walk into his arms, and I fall into his kiss as it becomes the only thing I can focus on.

'This is so beautiful; I can't believe you organised all this.'

'This is only the beginning.'

There's a knock on the door; Petra glides in, and Cody asks me to sit down.

Petra puts two plates in front of us.

I laugh.

Our first course is mac and cheese bites. We also have two plastic wine glasses, and Petra fills them up with sparkling water.

When she leaves us again, Cody and I chat until she comes back with our main course. We never run out of things to say. We end up talking about tuis in kowhai trees, tornadoes and Mt Cook.

When I see our main course, it makes me laugh out loud. Coleslaw, fish, and chips. All of our dinner has come from the local fish and chip shop.

Petra clears everything away, and we start eating again, fish and chips on a plate with knives and forks surrounded by rose petals and candles. That's a novel experience and has to have been my best birthday ever.

The next time Petra comes back, she hands Cody a gift and clears our plates. Cody stands up and walks me to the front of the surf tower where the sun is setting, painting the sky in pinks like my dress. I open my gift as he holds me from behind, nibbling on my neck.

A Pandora bracelet with five charms on it. A horse, cow, surfboard, flower, and a cake.

He puts the bracelet on me, and we kiss until Petra arrives with the dessert. Cinnamon and sugar doughnuts. She tops up our sparkling water one last time, and after we finish, we stroll off down the beach to burn off some of those calories.

When we get back, the tower is a lifeguard tower again. No candles in sight. Sadly,

Cody and I then have to go our separate ways. But it's not long till we are together again in my dreams, walking in the sand, laughing in the sunshine, and never letting go of each other unless we are surfing perfect waves.

It honestly has been the perfect birthday.

Christmas

Christmas Eve, we finish our shifts and rush to our work meeting in the hall.

'Quieten down you lot!' Mark calls over all the post shift chatter.

'Listen up.'

'Will do.' Api calls out.

'Shhh.' Meg laughs.

Then we all laugh.

'Shall I donate your hampers to the Raglan surf life savers instead?' Mark calls and we all quieten. Nothing like beach rivalry to focus us.

'The local businesses have put together a hamper for each of you to say *thanks for keeping the community safe.*'He lifts a sheet on a table and there are brown giftbags with a Pohutukawa tree stamped on them. Mark wishes us Merry Christmas and gives us our hampers. As I leave, I look in my bag, a bottle of wine, soaps, locally made chocolate and a Ngaruma Bay anthology to read.

Afterwards, Cody walks me to my car, lit up by a glorious yellow and orange sunset. There is a horrible metre distance between us, so we don't look like a couple. I just want one last touch or kiss, but I guess I'll have to wait.

'Sandy, let's celebrate Christmas together on Boxing Day,' he says over our metre gap.

'Okay.' I open my boot to put my bags in and leave his wrapped gift in there.

'See you after Christmas,' he drives off and I follow and laugh at him, dancing as he drives, and making funny gestures to me. I return them as I sing, this time to Christmas music putting me in the festive spirit.

It's dark when I pull into the long, winding gravel driveway, and all my family is waiting for me under the full moon.

'About bloody time,' James says.

'No gifts till Sandra arrives,' Chris mimics Mum.

Mum throws a tea towel at Chris. He catches it and chases the others around, whipping them with it.

'Are you lot seven or seventeen?' I laugh. 'Would be nice to be welcomed home with love – not greed.'

'I agree.' Mum wraps her arms around me. 'I give you all love, no greed.'

'Me too.' Dad gives my hair a scuffle. It was plaited nicely, but he totally ruins it. That's why I never have nice hair.

'Glad you missed me.' I snuggle under Dad's musky smelling armpit.

We chat about what I've been up to, until we all sit in the lounge around the Christmas tree. I love the pine smell of Christmas. Dad's always so excited about the Christmas tree as he grows them on the farm, just for this season.

We have a tradition where we open one present under the tree on Christmas Eve. The present I choose to open is big and squishy. An oversized hoody with warm, fluffy fabric on the inside. That will come in handy on the nights at the beach. Then we all get our Christmas Eve book and snuggle in a quiet reading spot. My spot is always close to the green, red and gold-decorated tree, on the floor, leaning back on Dad's knees. My book this year is Sasha A Linderson *When the rain falls*. I am instantly hooked and sad when I have to put it down for bed an hour later.

Finally, I slide in between my holly-printed Christmas sheets. So nice to sleep in my own bed again. I fall asleep the minute my head hits the pillow. I don't stay awake listening for Santa's sleigh bells as I used to on Christmas Eve. Funnily enough, I often heard them, too.

Christmas Day is busy from the minute my feet fall out of bed. It always is. My cousin and her parents arrive before breakfast, and our two families start making meals.

My auntie, mum, and cousin are busy with me in the kitchen. The boys and Dad are digging up potatoes and harvesting peas along with the normal farm jobs.

We are not sexist. I can do every job they do on the farm, just the boys can't prepare meals as good as us, and they can't fold serviettes in the shape of fans for the table. So, we do the jobs we prefer. When the meal's prepared for cooking, we stop for a champagne breakfast and get to open one more gift each.

I hand out my gifts to everyone. They all love their screen-printed art on a tee-shirt, sweatshirt, or shopping bag of our private family beach with the words *Welch's Surf* under the print. I even get requests for more.

After breakfast, my fingers go back to peeling spuds and shelling peas, and when everything is prepared, simmering, roasting, and the table's set, it is time for the highlight of the day—the gifts!

My job as the baby of the family is to hand out the presents. It's a long time before I get to open anything myself, but I love to watch the others open theirs as I pass them out. Watching their excited faces *means* Christmas to me. Mum always says Christmas is the gift of giving. I definitely feel that way.

Finally, I open mine. Some incredible clothes and even some makeup, a gardening kit, a cake decorating set, and a new surfboard. I also get a new CD from my favourite band, the Seagulls.

We are eating dinner when James comes out with another gift for me. 'It's from Cody.'

I have made him a tee and hoodie screen-printed with our beach – to remember me when he's back in the city. But I haven't given it to him yet. I've also done a painting of the beach we had our first date on.

Slowly, I unwrap Cody's gift, wishing he was here. Oh my gosh, it's a jewellery box the colour of the ocean with shells glued on it. The bottom says *Made with love for Sandy by Cody.* 'Oh.'

James snickers. Mum also says, 'Ohh.'

I open the box to see the inside, and there is a smaller gift. I unwrap that, and it's a ring box. Opening that box, I see a beautiful silver ring with a blue gem on it. I love it so much and instantly put it on. It fits my right-hand ring finger perfectly. The boys tease me about how much Cody likes me. I hope they are right.

Boxing Day, I'm on the afternoon shift, so I don't have to race back to work. But I get there thirty minutes before my shift. Cody's waiting for me.

We quickly walk along to the dunes before our shift starts, but we only get there in time to turn around – no kissing.

As soon as our shift finishes, we have our Christmas in the clubhouse. Everybody is back for it, we exchange gifts. Ryder puts his hoodie on, smiling. Hopefully, he likes it. And I get a beach towel with a lifeguard tower on it.

Cody and I stay behind to clean up when everyone heads off to bed. I finally give him his gift; he's already seen the ring on me and has been playing with it on my finger when we've been alone.

'This ring is beyond amazing – thank you so much.'

'Suits you.' He unwraps my gift. But I distract him with a kiss.

Once we break apart, he opens my painting of us surfing the waves the day we met. I painted it in watercolours and even drew the stick in the breaking waves. He is blown away. 'I didn't know you could paint.'

Then he opens my screen-printed tops. Straight away, he puts the hoodie on and says he loves them.

Sadly, we have to go off to bed after that, as we are on the morning shift the next day.

Famous

We're working in the sweltering sun when I spot the lead singer from the Seagulls, picnicking at the beach with his family. Our whole family love them, and we have even seen them perform live.

I'm working, while he's holidaying, so I try to treat him no differently from everyone else at the beach.

'Would you please stop perving? Your boyfriend is beside you. That old dude has a wife and kids,' Cody mutters. Bugger, he has noticed me staring.

I look at Cody. He doesn't know who the man is.

Petra comes over and spots the man I can't take my eyes off. 'Ffarrrr out!'

'What?' Cody asks.

I wink at Petra.

Cody heads off before we can explain, kicking the sand – that mad habit that he has. We all laugh, but I need to chase him down to explain. It's annoying that he's being jealous. As *if* I would flirt with some other guy – and a married man at that – when I've got Cody as a boyfriend. How can he not get that? Before I can run after him, he returns with Api, who says, 'Dude, look who's over there?'

'Who?' Cody's face is the colour of our uniforms.

Api looks over and laughs. 'Cody, do you live under a shell or something?'

'What?' Cody asks.

'You're safe. Sandra's not checking him out.'

'I might be,' I laugh.

'Come on,' Petra says to me, and I follow her down to the beach. We both laugh, leaving Api to explain who the Seagulls are to Cody.

As we are coming back, Brayden, the lead singer, is rocking his baby, trying to stop him from crying. He and his wife are also trying to calm their baby girl, and they have missed that their little boy has run into the water.

'Whoaaa,' I call out. The young boy is too close to the waves. I sprint on the sand, trying to get his attention and scoop him up just before he gets bowled over by an upcoming wave.

Brayden runs to us and scoops his son into his arms. 'Thanks,' he says to me.

'You're welcome, anytime. Enjoy your outing.'

New Year' Eves

The week between Christmas and New Year's is like most other weeks – I'm over hiding my relationship with Cody. Several other relationships have formed within the group, and at evening games, they hold each other tight.

I want Cody to hold me somewhere other than the dunes – even though we've started to go there at every possible chance.

I love kissing him, but having him claim me is all I want now. I know he's mine constantly. Unless he's in his uniform, he only wears the clothes I made him for Christmas.

The other thing is Nina is back. She hasn't talked to Cody, as far as I know. But she's still watching him.

At the close of the shift before New Year's Eve, all of us life savers head to the clubhouse for a meeting with Shane. 'The beach is a no-alcohol zone from November to February, and every time we see anyone with alcohol, we confiscate it. Once a year, we are allowed to drink the drinks we've confiscated. And that is New Year's Eve.'

Cheers fill the room.

'We have to choose four of us to be sober. Come pick straws. If you get a shorty, you're one of the four lifesavers on duty.'

I'm next to Cody. He has a long straw and will be drinking. I don't want to. I've drunk a few times, but in that situation, I'd fall all over Cody – that wouldn't be good. Even worse is if we both were drunk, so when Alex, who is next to me, gets a short straw and is disappointed, I subtly swap my straw with her, volunteering to be sober. Meg, Petra, and another guy I don't know very well are with me on sober duty.

The night of the countrywide party, we four sober lifeguards walk around taking lots of alcohol from people partying at the beach and keeping them under control, but we also pop up in pairs to the clubhouse to join parts of the party with our fellow Lifesavers.

At about 11 o'clock at night, Petra and I go to the clubhouse for our turn. I scan the room for the tee or hoodie that I made Cody, but I can't see them or him amongst the swaying teens. I dance with Tyson until Ryder tries to get me to team up with him playing darts.

That's when I see Ryder's sister, clearly drunk, stumbling out of the men's toilets, buttoning her sheer white shirt up and grinning.

A minute later, Cody walks out, and he looks around to see if anyone has seen him.

My blood boils. I duck behind Ryder, so Cody doesn't see me, then sneak into the men's toilet myself. I need to know if anyone else is in there. Empty. So, they had been alone. I leave the toilet, swallowing my tears and gripping anger in the palm of my hands. I hold my head high, charging towards the clubhouse exit, taking off my jewellery while I escape.

As I pass Cody, I shove all the jewellery he has given me into his hand and say, 'Stay.

Away. From. Me.' I leave before I can see his reaction or give him a chance to explain.

Once outside, I run under the tower. I can still work, keep an eye out, but no one can see me here. That's a lie – how can I work? I can't see beyond the uncontrollable tears escaping out my eyes; like a broken dam, they have become crashing rivers. My body ripples as warm drops flow onto the sand.

My first relationship has just ended. My world has ended. Mum and Dad love him, my brothers love him, I love him. But it's wasted love.

My friend once dated one twin, Tony, and they broke up after six months. They were both sad for a while, and they even tried to get back together, but it still didn't work. I guess Cody still likes Nina, or he is upset I'm not putting out. I'm glad I didn't give myself to him – especially now that he's cheated on me. I wish I'd never met him.

'Petra,' I hear Cody call out.

'How drunk are you?' Petra laughs at him. 'Can't be drunk on the beach – go back inside.'

'I just sobered up real quick,' Cody says.

'What's wrong?' Petra asks.

'Fucking Nina, I hate her,' he says.

'Join the club,' Petra says. 'What did she do this time?'

'She followed me into the toilets, and when I came out, she was standing there naked.'

'Did you cheat on Sandra?'

'No, never!' he hisses. 'I locked myself in the toilet cubicle and told her to leave. Before she left, she said everyone thinks we are together, and we should be.'

'Did Sandra see?'

'She must have.' Cody sniffs.

'Oh shit,' Petra says. 'But you swear you didn't do anything?'

I can't see what he has done. Maybe he shows her the jewellery or simply shakes his head. Or maybe he cries more. Either way, Petra gets the idea.

But do I believe him? I saw the smug look on Nina's face.

'No way! She's psycho.'

'What the fuck, Cody?' Tyson comes running over closer.

'Nothing happened,' Cody says quickly.

'I saw Nina walking out of the toilet with an *I got screwed* look on her face, buttoning up her top. We all saw her grinning like the cat who got the fucking cream. I want to bloody well hit you.'

'I swear I didn't even touch her. She was naked, so I locked myself in the cubicle till she'd gone.'

'Sure didn't look that way to me! Where's Sandra?'

'We don't know.' Petra says.

'Bastard,' Tyson adds, running off.

'I didn't... I would never,' Cody calls after him.

Cody walks off, and Petra heads to the other sober lifeguards to tell them some tale about why I'm missing. When she comes back down, I say, only loud enough for her to hear me,

'I'm still here and still working, but I won't talk to anyone. Sorry, that includes you.'

'He loves you,' she says.

I'm over talking and pull my legs up to my chest and snuggle them like a teddy bear, my chest beating throughout my sobs.

Cody comes back after a while.

'I can't find her. What if she's hurt?'

'She's not. She just doesn't want to see you.'

'Cody,' Nina calls, walking his way.

'Fuck off, Nina, I don't like you! I wouldn't screw someone drunk in the toilets. Stop implying we are together. Just fuck off and leave me alone.' Cody screams at her.

'Please, Cody, give me one more chance.'

Like Cody, I can hear Nina crying.

'Fuck off! Nina, I don't like you!' Cody yells.

'Nina, when did you last make out with Cody in reality?' Petra asks.

'Last year,' Nina says.

'A kiss on the forehead doesn't count, Nina,' Cody spits.

'Two years ago, tonight,' Nina admits.

'If you really like Cody, why are you wrecking his summer?' Petra calls. 'Let him be. He doesn't like you.'

I accept that Cody hasn't cheated on me. But I still don't want to see him.

The feelings I had when I thought he'd cheated were horrible. Is that what heartbreak feels like? I never want to feel like that again. I don't want to let Cody near me again if he can make me hurt like this.

When the fireworks explode, I stay in my hiding spot. The singing starts, and I'm still there when it ends. The beach is clear of people, and the surf club emptied and closed for the night.

I stay where I am, and somewhere during the night, I fall asleep.

When I jolt awake, it's so dark. No stars to be seen and a chill in the air. I'm busting, and my mouth's dry.

I run to the dorms and freshen up before I wriggle into bed.

'You okay?' Petra mumbles.

'Night,' I reply.

I'm so glad she takes the hint.

I have the next day off, so I get up early and drive home. But halfway there, I decide I can't tell my family. They all love Cody – why is he so amazing?

Instead, I make the mistake of turning off to the beach where Cody and I had our first surf.

I walk past the spot Cody and I had fooled around at and stroll as far as I can before lying down and trying to sort my life out some more.

Then I move the sand around. Forming a turret, a bridge, a moat. Before I know it, I have made a big sand sculpture.

As a family, we often have sand sculpting competitions, and I win almost every time. Maybe working for the holidays has been a mistake. Maybe I should go home. A break in the natural beach noises makes me look up.

The twins walk towards me. 'Boy, have you worried a lot of people today.' Tony says.

'You, okay?' Richard asks.

I start crying again, and they both run to hold me.

'Why do people start relationships when they hurt this much as they collapse?' I sob.

'He doesn't want to end things with you. He swears he didn't cheat.'

'I know, I believe him, but I never want to feel like this again. I don't think I can go back to him,' I say.

That's when I hear a thud. I look through my tears to see Cody's here, too. He's sobbing, walking my way, kicking the sand, supported by James.

'I think he loves you,' Richard whispers as he stands and walks over to Cody.

He reaches out his hand and pulls Cody up. James follows, and together, my two brothers pull my ex-boyfriend over to me. This time, Cody sinks into the sand.

'I swear she didn't touch me; I only want you,' he sobs.

I don't want him to hurt me anymore, but I still like him so much and having him break down like this is too much. My tears match his. Shallow breaths in unison. Hands apart, but both shaking.

'I don't want the drama anymore,' I finally say.

'I never wanted it; I just want you.'

He reaches his hand towards my bare wrist and wraps his fingers around where his bracelets have been all summer.

'I am sorry, I'll tell her. I'll tell the entire world. Please be mine again. I am not me without you.'

'We are too young to fall apart like this,' I say. 'You are my first boyfriend. This relationship is too much.'

'Sandra,' Cody says. 'I'm sorry, but I have very serious thoughts about us and our relationship.'

'Our past relationship. Sorry, Cody. We are over.'

I walk away as Cody cries louder. All my brothers support him, traitors.

I walk out of sight and then cry again myself. I plan to quit my first job and head home tomorrow.

James runs up to me. 'Don't you like him?' he yells.

'I love him. I can't have someone have this effect on me. I can't handle feeling heartbroken. I would rather be single for the rest of my life than feel like this again.'

'Sandra, please give love a chance. I think you two have what Vanessa and I have. Not everyone gets to have this deep a connection with their partner.' James tells me.

'I don't want to experience this heartache.'

'It's like never going on a plane in case it might crash.'

'I don't like flying either.'

'Be sensible, Sandra. That man over there is probably your soulmate! He loves you, and he wants you, probably more than anyone else, and you're pushing him away because you don't want him to hurt you.'

James gets up and stomps away. He has never spoken to me like this. He's always been the one person in my corner, the one person who always has my back. I'm losing everyone. I burst into heavier tears. More so when Richard comes over to me. He wraps his arms around my body, and I let his hug engulf me.

Cody walks towards me and says, 'I'm sorry, Sandra. I don't want to be a clingy ex, so I'm gonna go and leave you to it.'

He turns and walks away.

Gone

He's gone. Cody is gone... I think I am going to vomit. This is so much more painful than the heartache from a misunderstanding. Have I lost him for good? I still want him. It all dawns on me. Cody and I are meant to be together! That's why it hurts so much.

I stand and chase after him, 'Cody!'

He turns.

I open my arms.

He charges at me. Cody is still crying, but his cries are more broken now as he lays in my arms while my brothers walk back down the beach, leaving us to it.

We don't talk, and I savour just holding him.

'I'm sorry,' he says.

'I'm sorry too. I do believe you,' I assure him.

He starts shaking and pulls away from me a little. 'I promise I didn't touch her; I haven't touched her or anyone but you in two years.'

'I know.' I don't know how I know, but I do. I know I can trust him.

'Can I please put these back on you?' he asks, pulling out my jewellery.

I nod.

He starts with the ring, then the bracelet, and finally the necklace.

'Is there anything else you want to put on me?' I ask.

'Many things,' he says, playing with my ring finger.

'Slow down, Cody. I meant your lips.'

'Sandra, will you please be mine? Let me be yours?'

'Yes, Cody. Kiss me already.'

He does, and we kiss until it starts to rain. My brothers announce their return with a cough, breaking us up.

'Are you okay if we head home now?' James asks.

'Thanks so much.' Cody gets up and hugs them all. I follow, thanking them.

'Don't tell Mum and Dad, please.'

'They know,' Tony says.

The five of us walk back to three cars.

We all get in our cars and drive.

Once back at the dorm, Cody sneaks in with me.

When we enter my room, he holds his hand up to his lips for Petra.

'Can I stay – I just want to hold her, please? I don't want to lose her.'

Petra nods, and Cody and I get into my bed, both fully dressed.

We are late waking the next morning, and as promised, we haven't even kissed, but he's held me all night.

From bed, we can hear Ariana and Nina talking.

'Cody and my break is almost over; I'm studying in the city this year, and I'll visit him there.'

Cody shakes his head at me.

Petra gets up when it sounds quiet and comes back, saying, 'The coast is clear.'

Cody sneaks out, and Petra comes back to me. In whispers, I update her.

Petra helps me with my makeup, and we leave the dorms for the day.

The boys are playing catch with a ball. Petra and I walk past them all and set the tower up.

Nina volunteers to work as someone in our team can't work our shift.

The workday is long and horrible. Cody spends most of his time out of the tower, like the rest of us, ignoring Nina.

We are quite rude, really.

We've had enough of her by the time our shift ends. Nina stays on shift, but the rest of us leave.

Once we change, we pick up the ball and walk up the beach a bit. As soon as we are far enough away, Cody slips his hand in mine.

I smile at him. I almost lost him, but here he is, still mine. We all throw the ball around for awhile and then go our own ways.

Cody and I head to our normal spot in the dunes. He's on top of me, and we deal with some of the tension from the last few days.

Cody is all over me. Like he can't get enough. Physically, he has taken things slowly with me – until now. Today he seems to have skipped some steps. One hand makes its way inside my top and his other one glides down the back of my shorts to my bottom, squishing it as he moves all around. I can feel he wants even more.

'Cody!' Nina screeches.

'Bugger off,' Cody says, still kissing me.

'So, you have moved on.'

'Fuck off,' Cody says again. 'This is an actual relationship, and I am sick of you causing me issues. Leave my girlfriend and me alone.'

Nina runs off crying.

'Cody,' I say.

'Fuck!' he says, rolling off me. 'She's ruined another day for us, hasn't she?'

'No,' I follow where he is lying on his back and climb on top of him. 'I don't want my first time to be in the sand dunes. I want it to be romantic. I think you were amping it up a tad more than normal.'

'I know! Sorry, I need to be closer to you.' He makes those puppy dog eyes at me. And he rolls so he's on top of me again.

'I know, I want it too, but let's make it special and not rush it, please.'

'Absolutely.' He rolls off me and takes a deep breath. We lie there holding hands and pointing out shapes in the clouds.

'Come on, guys.' Petra says, walking past us with the rest of the team.

We go back to playing ball and walking along the beach.

When we get back, Nina still hasn't let it sink in, and she comes up to Cody and says, 'We need to talk.'

'We have talked. You and I are over. You were never my girlfriend; you were just a fling, and I now have an amazing girlfriend. You need to stop. I'll never go back to you. I was never with you in the first place. It was a one-night stand, and you dreamt it into some make-believe relationship. If it was one, I would have called you, kissed you all the time. I did not do that because it was all in your fucking head. Leave me alone!' Cody runs off down the beach.

Nina runs off, too. In fact, she heads to her car and drives off.

Hurting

The next morning, as I start to walk towards Cody to meet him for our morning run, Ryder gets to him first.

The boys talk for a minute, then hug, and my heart sinks as I see Cody wipe away tears.

I go for my run alone. I guess some new Nina drama is going on, and he will tell me later if he needs me.

But both guys are gone when I come back from my run – in fact, they are gone for the rest of the day, as is Ariana, Nina's best friend. I want to message him, but I will not act that clingy – especially after New Year's.

As four of the eighteen of us are not here, and six are on their days away, most of us do a double shift. It's nice working with other people. I feel close to the team I normally work with but have not really gotten to know the others, and now I know them better – double shift in the scorching sun does that to a team.

One boy, Sandeep who has been talking to me a lot today makes a move on me. We're just being friendly, chatting, and I don't see it coming until he has his lips on mine.

I pull away. 'What are you doing?'

'Making my move finally.' He grins.

'No, I have a man,' I say.

'He doesn't have to know.' He puts his hand on mine. 'What happens at the beach – stays at the beach.'

I stand up, my insides rattling. 'Leave me alone, please.'

Petra walks over and puts her arm around me. 'Leave her alone, she's taken.'

Later that night, Ariana arrives back crying. I assume the two boys are back, too, but I give Cody some space.

The next morning, I take off on my run.

'Wait up,' Cody calls, joining me after five minutes.

'Hey,' I say, turning around.

'How was your day yesterday?' I ask, running beside him.

His face drops.

I stop running and hug him. 'You okay?'

'I'm not meant to tell anyone,' he murmurs.

'Well, you shouldn't then, as long as you are alright.'

'This is why I love you so much. Any other girl would press me.'

'Love?' I question.

'Oops,' he says with a timid smile, 'but yeah, I think you're amazing. Every day, you surprise me like this.'

'Shall we just walk today?' I ask.

'You know what? Let's run.'

And he runs the fastest and hardest I've ever seen him run. Even I can't keep up.

We have the early shift, and Ryder has swapped a shift with Rose to give her a break after the double.

It's interesting having Ryder be the only one who doesn't know about Cody and me, and all he does is ask Cody about his girlfriend.

The two have been best friends over the last two summers and have even hung out between summers, but they have hardly seen each other this year.

'So, tell me all about your girlfriend? What's she like?'

'She's sandy,' he says.

'What?' Ryder looks at Cody like Cody has lost the plot.

'She's always covered in sand from the beach,' Cody adds, cracking up.

I just about choke laughing.

'Why don't you bring her here?'

'Cause of Nina, she was full-on.'

'Fair point,' he says. 'Well, Nina won't be back here for ages; you should invite her to the bonfire.'

'I will next week,' he says. Cody tells the others all about my family and farm and how much he loves it at my place and can't wait to go back there.

I tell the others about my brother's engagement and how it happened.

And then, much to everyone's surprise, Ryder tells us about Nina. 'Please don't tell anyone this,' Ryder starts, 'but yesterday, Nina tried to take her own life.'

The mood changes instantly.

'Oh Ryder,' the girls take turns hugging him.

I slide over to Cody and hug him. 'So sorry, are you ok?'

'Yeah.'

'We visited her last night and are going to see her today.'

'I don't like her,' Petra says bluntly, 'but I wouldn't wish that on -anyone. I hope she gets better, Ryder.'

'She's ok; she may have even faked it. It wouldn't be the first time,' he says with a glance at Cody.

I'm still holding Cody, but as the girls are holding Ryder, it doesn't look out of place.

'But she is getting the help she needs,' Cody adds.

'That's good,' we all say in different ways.

After that, I escape out on patrol. The atmosphere in the room is too dark for such a sunny day. I need time to sort myself out. I feel so bad – like I've caused it. I know I haven't, but I've contributed to Nina being so sad. And I bet Cody feels like I do, but much worse. He snapped at her. He was nice to start with, but she wouldn't listen.

I look out at the waves and focus on their crashing, pushing Nina and the drama that circles her out of my mind. I decide to have a surf after this shift.

Cody catches up with me patrolling the sand.

I say, 'That's heavy,'

'Yeah, she's a very complicated person. When we got there, her parents were mad at me, but we sat down with a nurse, and I told them my side of the story. They could see how Nina had manipulated everything. Medical records proved Nina was never actually pregnant.'

'Oh Cody, she made you go through the loss of a child for nothing?' I feel tears falling down my cheeks. I don't mean to cry, but Nina has put Cody through so much.

At that, he starts to cry, too, and I hold him. 'I never told anyone about that child, but I planted a tree for him or her at the park across the road from my apartment. I've been leaving flowers there often, and it was all for nothing.'

I let him cry it out before asking, 'What did her parents say to you?'

'Her parents were shocked at all she's done to me, and I told them I have a lovely girl now, but how Nina is not accepting it.

We are going back to see her today after the shift, but that will be the last time I visit her.'

That afternoon I have to myself, and I go surfing. It's a great chance to reflect on everything. I've gone from living a very sheltered life at home to going skinny dipping, seeing some awful truths about manipulation and how someone can hurt herself and others with such horrific lies. All of this world is beyond what I've ever experienced before – beyond what I thought I'd learn at a simple surf lifesaving job.

The girl, Alex, whom I swapped my short straw on New Year's Eve with, swims over and surfs with me.

I've not spoken to her before our double shifts yesterday, but we have lots in common. We hang out for the rest of the day.

'I like Ryder. But he seems like anyone's.'

'He's put himself out there,' I say.

'I don't know if I want to be the next fling or if I should wait till next year – he may calm down.'

'Or he may be taken.'

'True. Better to love and lose than not to love at all.'

I think back to when I thought I'd lost Cody. I guess she has a point.

'Do you like anyone?'

Why not – I thought. 'Yeah – Cody.'

Her reaction surprises me. 'You and Cody are like magnets. The way you move around each other, and he's always watching you. He goes on about his girlfriend and how amazing she is, and you can tell in his eyes he really means it, but then when you are near, it's all about you.'

'Wow, you are observant,' I say.

'What does that mean?' she asks.

'I am his girlfriend.'

'What?' Her eyes light up. 'That's perfect!'

'We haven't been able to say anything because of Nina.'

'Fair enough. That girl is crazy.'

'Will you keep my secret?'

'Sure.' She smiles.

Not long after, Ryder and Cody come walking down the beach and sit with us.

'Why don't the four of us go out for dessert?' I say, looking in the direction of the ice cream shop down the beach.

'I have never been there,' Alex says.

'Me either,' I hold back my grin, knowing that Alex is scheming.

'Sounds great.' Ryder gets up, brushing sand off his board shorts.

'Alex guessed about us,' I say to Cody as we trail behind Alex and Ryder.

He laughs, slipping his hand into mine. 'Ryder did, too.' 'I missed you today,' he tells me.

'I had a great day surfing,' I say.

He responds by kissing me.

'Maybe I missed you a little bit.' I laugh, and we kiss more.

The other two turn to face us and clap.

Cody does a fake bow and says, 'As you were.'

'Alex likes Ryder!' I whisper to Cody.

We have a great night. After sharing ice cream sundaes, the boys take us to a freshwater pool with a waterfall. Another new experience.

We don't have togs, so again, we wait until it's dark. Cody and I make out a bit while the other two get to know each other.

'We haven't been able to be like this before,' Cody says to the others when we come up for air. 'There was always someone around.'

'What about at the farm?'

'No, I have four brothers and overprotective parents,' I say.

'Cool, go for it. We're having a great time by ourselves over here,' Ryder says, moving closer to Alex.

The next time we come up for air, they are kissing too, and it's almost dark enough to go skinny dipping under the waterfall in the moonlight. It's an amazing experience, but it's freezing.

The last time we skinny-dipped, I'd been shy, and Cody had been full-on. This time, I know he's experienced, and he knows I'm not.

He stays close but not touching me.

'You can hold me,' I say.

'Can I?' he asks.

'Yes,' I say, pulling him to me, kissing with even more passion.

But the other two seem to be moving faster than us. The next day, we have our last shift before heading off to the farm.

Alex and Ryder are officially together and all over each other.

Is there a doctor in the house?

We arrive at the farm just before dinner. I get on with my chores, and Dad has some jobs set for Cody. Cody handles himself around Dad surprisingly well.

If Cody and I break up for real, whoever I bring home next will have a hard act to follow, assuming I ever got over him, that is.

It is just the four of us for tea. The working bee is in a couple of days, but our time off was earlier, so we will start renovating tomorrow.

Everyone goes to bed early and gets up early. I do the chickens and the stables before anyone else is up. I can hear Dad awake, listening to Newstalk on the radio, which is how he always likes to start his day.

Cody is next up, and we go for a quick 45-minute horse ride. It's only his second time on a horse. 'I'll be glad if I don't fall off.' He grips on tight.

I take him on a ride around the farm, showing him all the houses and possible building platforms.

'Wow,' he says. 'Your brothers told me guys are waiting to date you, and they didn't want to let them. Do they all know about this?'

'Yip, and one even joked he would marry me for the farm. I got so upset I poured juice all over him.'

'Good on you.'

We start working at the house after breakfast.

It's worse than I remembered. We have a plan to start and finish one room at a time so we can see progress, so we start in the kitchen. By the end of the day, the cabinets are ready to be painted, and the walls are too. Even the lino is lifted. That was like peeling glue off your skin – strangely rewarding. Tomorrow, the room can be painted and will be done. We even strip the laundry next door.

The following day, we get into painting, and in between coats, we start working outside, pulling out weeds so we don't stir up any dust inside.

'I guess with family close by, it will be easy for them to get babysitters,' Cody says as we work.

'Sure, will be. I'll be the first one offering. I love babies.'

'Me too.'

The next day, we strip the lounge and hall, and then the others arrive.

James and Vanessa are so excited to see the progress we've made.

After tea, we all go up the road to the pub. This is the first time I'm allowed to go, but only because Mum and Dad are here.

At one stage, Cody and I are alone at the table. We sneak a kiss, and a friend of the twins comes up to Cody, warning him not to touch me.

My brothers race back in no time, explaining Cody is my boyfriend.

'But I have been waiting for her my whole life,' Angus says.

'You said we had to wait till she was eighteen,' another school mate complains.

I had no idea anyone from school liked me. To me, they were just my brothers' best friends. Maybe this is a joke. Either way, it's all too much.

Cody and I slip out the back door, and Dad drives us home.

I'm so embarrassed, I just sit in the back seat with Mum's arm around me and cry.

I don't know why I cry so much. Maybe it's the exhaustion of all the hard work after an emotional week of lifesaving.

I don't talk to Cody again that night and see him the next morning when I've calmed down. This time, he is up earlier than me, and we enjoy a morning run before doing my farm jobs. I start with the chickens. We don't talk about the night before.

There are many people to feed for the next day. Vanessa's family join our family, and together, we all work hard at the house, stripping the rest of the inside and gardening outside.

One of her cousins is a tiler, and another a plumber. James is studying to be an electrician, and some of his friends come over, and they all sort the wires out.

Pavers are laid, walls painted, wires connected, and by the end of the day, the difference is amazing.

Cody asks me what the arch at the end of the garden overlooking the beach is for. I explain to him that was where James popped the question, and they would get married, have their children's baptisms, and pictures of first days of school there under the arch. He is in awe.

I walk Cody back to the main house and kiss him goodbye. 'See you tomorrow.'

He's about to go when there's a commotion in the house. We run back inside to see what's happened.

'Tony has cut his finger off,' Richard yells as he paces the lounge.

Cody turns and runs back to our kitchen.

I don't know what he is doing, but I can hear a lot of panic and yelling from my family. Mum is sitting on the couch, silent. I hold her.

Vanessa is on the floor in front of her fiancé. It's not just the blood and the finger that's causing the panic – it's his voice, the gurgling scream that's hissing between his teeth.

Cody walks into the lounge. He has ice and a container. He places the severed finger on ice and clips up the lid.

'It's his right arm – how will he write?' Mum cries.

Everyone watches Cody. Once all the panic has calmed down a little, we are told the local doctor is on his way.

'Do you know what I love most about this family?' Cody says as we see the doctor's car pull up. We all look dumbfounded.

'You all ask so many questions of me, and know so much, but no one has asked what I am studying to be. I am a third-year medical student. So, I have my advantages in situations like this,' he says, winking at me.

I can't believe I never asked that. 'Sorry, I should have asked about your study.' I feel so ashamed.

'No, Sandy, it's a good thing. You are not pretentious or with me just because I am going to be a doctor.'

'You two are not with each other for anything but good reasons,' Mum says. 'I hope we see a lot more of you, Cody. Thanks for helping us this weekend with the house and the finger.'

Cody speaks to the ambulance officers, telling them about what he's done, and he hands them Tony's finger on ice.

Vanessa's family is packing up back at what will become her home.

The rest of us stand around Cody's car to farewell him and thank him for his quick moves to save the finger.

I kiss him when we are alone.

'Next weekend, can we go to your place?' I ask.

'I would love that,' he says, 'but this here, where we are now, has more love and spirit than anywhere else I've ever been.'

'Thanks, I love you,' I say to him.

'I love you too.' We kiss again.

'That's enough,' Mum says, coming back out.

I'm sad to see him disappear around the corner in our driveway. I love having him with me in my world, and I feel like he belongs here. But I do think it's time I get to know his world.

After we've packed up and eaten lasagna for dinner, made from Betsy, our old cow, we drive into town.

Angus

Saturday night, and the boys want a beer. After the previous night at the pub, I'm not keen, but I go anyway.

One guy, Angus Johnston, sticks to me like glue. He has been Tony's best friend at school and is always over at our house – like a cousin. He keeps talking about how he's almost finished at vet school and loves our farm. I'm not really paying too much attention – dreaming about riding waves with Cody's perfect white teeth smiling between breaks.

'Mum, I want to go home please. It's been a long day. I'll just use the girl's room; then can we go?'

'Sure thing,' she says.

Angus follows me in. 'How can you do this, Sandra? Embarrass me like that.'

'Umm, this is the woman's loos.' I don't know what he's on about.

'Parading around with another man. You are mine.' He yells, reaching out and pulling my shirt so tight that I lose my balance and a few of the buttons.

Swaying, I regain my footing and reach into the back pocket of my jeans, dialing the police.

He takes my hands out, knocking my phone to the ground, and holds them both above my head with one hand as he pulls so the rest of the buttons pop and the blue fabric tears. 'Our first time was not meant to be like this, but you have given me no choice. You need to be punished.'

He bites my neck and then licks down my front where he's torn my bra.

With a thundering heartbeat and taut muscles, I fight all his actions off as best as I can.

'I only went to vet school to gain skills for our farm. You and me, our future babies.'

I have no words, just tears which flow down my face. He licks them away before forcing his tongue inside my mouth.

As he starts down my front again, I vomit all over his head.

'You bitch, you will pay for that.' He screams, pulling me by my hair to the taps, where he begins washing the vomit off.

'Help,' I scream, finding my voice finally. 'Please, help me!'

He pulls my jeans down to rip my underwear off.

'Stop!' the police push the door open. I crumble to the floor. I'm grateful the police arrived before he did what he was seconds away from doing.

The twins arrive and try to punch Angus while the police are dragging him away. More police hold my brothers back from Angus.

Mum arrives, and I collapse, knowing she will stay by my side. Her trembling arms massage my shoulders as Dad carries me to a waiting ambulance. The rest of the night is a blur. I wake up the next day in Mum's bed, crying. I stay in there all day.

Vanessa visits and reads Harry Potter to me for a while before she brings up the subject.

'Hey honey, you okay?'

I shake my head.

'I know.' She puts her arm around me and hands me an enormous bar of chocolate. From the crocheted bag I made her last Christmas, she pulls out an adult colouring-in book with colouring pencils.

Without talking, we open to a random page and start colouring in together.

'You don't have to say anything, but I want to tell you that the police found out that Angus's dad has been abusing his mum – not that that makes it okay, but he's had a very screwed up childhood – unless he's been here. I guess that's why he fantasised you were a couple. And why he snapped. Angus's reasoning was he only did what he did because that's how his dad had taught him. The police are looking into his family.'

James pops in and out, joining us when he isn't helping Mum and Dad. 'Sandra, we have arranged a restraining order...he was charged with assault and attempted rape... he has to stay away from you and the farm. His mum and sister – they were both covered in bruises, too. They've left town for a safe new start in life.'

I'm too shaken to function. Sad for them – angry at him – relieved I won't have to see them again.

I feel so sad that Mrs Johnson has had what I experienced last night and more. I have a safe place to recover and get away. His mum had to live with it. She was a great postie. I wonder who will deliver the mail now? Glad she's safe. And what if she had stood up for herself and showed Angus it wasn't right? Maybe he wouldn't have hurt me. My hand softly brushes over the bruises on my face, the bite marks on my neck. 'His dad is horrible for letting him think he can treat women like this.' My voice is raspy, but Vanessa hears me, as her tears fall on the paper.

We watch a handful of 80's musicals as we colour more, serious chats over for now.

James stays with me at night, in my room.

I call in sick for my next shift. When I finally venture outside, the sun helps. Not sure if it helps the bruises on my skin or my heart. I garden and talk lots to the horses. The twins take me to the beach, and we surf for half an hour – but that's all I can manage. It does help, though.

Rainbow

After my third day off sick, Cody shows up to check on me. The last I'd seen, my phone was broken on the pub's toilet floor, so I've not even messaged him – not that I know what to say.

When he arrives, I collapse into his arms, covering his muscular shoulders with tears.

'What happened?'

My lip curls up. I can't tell him. He has already been through too much with Nina.

'Please, Sandy,' he nuzzles his nose into my hair.

Mum enters, 'Sandra, go have a shower, wash the garden dirt off yourself.

Cody doesn't care about the dirt, but it's Mum's way of giving me some space so she can tell Cody what's happened to me. The relief of not having to find the words myself is huge. I will love my mother forever.

When I reappear, Cody is wiping tears off his face. The second he spots me, his face crumples with anguish.

'Come on, beautiful,' he says, reaching out to me.

He gives me a gentle kiss on the cheek and says, 'I will always be here for you.'

'I know, I just didn't want to upset you. You've been through enough this summer.'

'You are more important to me than any of that.'

'Sorry.' I snuggle into him more. He picks me up and carries me to the barn, where he places me on a horse with help from Tony. And we trot off through the farm. He almost falls off, so for the first time in days, I laugh.

'That's better.' He grins at me.

We stop at the run-down house on the farm.

'Can we look inside?' he asks me.

We slide off the horses and tie them up.

Walking hand in hand, we step up to the broken wooden verandah.

'Stop!' Cody says suddenly. He scoops me up in his arms again.

'Just in case we ever live here.' He carries me over the threshold. Again, I laugh.

Cody calls in sick and has the remainder of his shifts this week away from surf club, too. He stays by my side unless we are sleeping.

We've both enjoyed restoring James's house together, so we look around the abandoned house. What could we do here? So much!

We clean it, and I leave the farm for the first time that week to go to the junkyard and get second-hand wood panels and windows. It's great having a project to keep our minds busy.

On the weekend, all the boys come back home, and they help us with the house. No one can believe the work we've already put into it. Days later, the walls are weatherproof, and the gardens cleared.

Cody and I have had no make-out sessions. I'm worried he doesn't want me now. But he holds me in support and gives me small kisses often as we talk about our future, so I don't push it. We have both been through a lot recently.

As the sun slides away on the last night before we are due to go back to the beach, Mum makes us a picnic dinner, and we have it by candlelight in the house we have been renovating.

'We need to name this cottage.' Cody says between bites.

'Like Shell Cottage?'

'No, something more specific and special.'

I stand up and look around and out the window I see a broken bench seat being overgrown with clumps of beautiful white lilies.

'How about Lily Cottage?' I say.

He stands behind me and wraps his arms tight. 'What about Lily Hill?'

'Yes, it's perfect.' I can see it all in my mind. A path and seats between the lilies. Lily patterned plates and maybe even wallpaper or cushions.

For half of our relationship, I have waited for him to make the first move. We are alone in this house, so it's now or never. Once we finish eating dinner, I pull out a pack of cards. 'Want to play a game?'

'What are you up to?' he laughs, looking sideways at me.

'Nothing, I just want to see more of you.

'I want to see more of you, too. We will see each other over winter, I promise.'

I deal a hand of poker. We play, and I throw the first game without him knowing.

Then I take off my top.

He has seen me in togs before, but not a lacy white bra like I'm wearing.

'What the.....?'

'Your deal,' I wink at him.

We play again, but this time I kick his arse. I knew I would.

'Whatcha taking off?' I ask.

He puts his hands on the bottom of his shirt and lifts it slowly. So slowly, I want to scream, 'Take it off!'

'Hello, six-pack, you got a gym in your apartment block?' I ask him.

'Why, yes, I do.' He flexes his arms. 'I work out while I study.'

We play again, and he loses and loses till he is down to just his boxer shorts.

We play one more time, and I let him win. I take my shorts off, showing him my matching undies that Alex and Petra helped me shop for.

Crawling around the blanket like a cat, I pounce on him.

I instantly know he still finds me attractive.

We haven't long been kissing when I hear my brother Chris's voice. 'Do you think we should warn them we are coming? What if they are, you know, doing it?'

'Well then, I'll shoot him.' I hear dad say.

It has taken me almost an hour to get Cody's clothes off him, but he is dressed within seconds, and we are playing Last Card by the time they walk in the door.

'This place looks great,' Richard says, and he takes a photo of us having our romantic picnic.

'There's still a lot of work on the roof to do.' We laugh as there is no roof or ceiling yet.

Dad says, 'I'll keep an eye out for tiles for you.'

The next morning, as we are about to leave, Cody asks me to go for a walk with him.

'If we end up living here,' he says, walking around the outside of the house, 'where do you want the arch for your proposal?' my stomach floats away with the clouds. A proposal – wow. I turn around, taking in the farm, garden, lilies, and sea view around the property.

'Here,' I say, standing in a spot where you can look down to the beach below, but in the opposite direction, you can see all the houses, the animals, and the stables. Cody walks away from me with a spade in his hand and digs a hole on either side. Then he tucks into a shed and reappears with two beautiful standard white roses and places them in each hole. 'I hope to marry you here one day, Sandra,' he says, kissing me. 'And these roses will be in bloom, and it will be a magical day. As magical as someone like you deserves.'

Mum comes up and starts helping us. There is a hedge of white roses planted there before the sun hides behind the clouds, and they are naturally watered.

'Next time, we will add the arch,' he says. Ducking for cover under Mum's umbrella.

'Cody, if we get married, there's no guarantee that this broken-down house will be ours. Four houses, five kids,' I say.

'This is your house if you want it,' Dad says, coming around the side of the shed, water dripping off his brimmed hat. 'You have put all the love into renovating it, and

I think it's going to be the most magnificent one.

We all stand on the spot and take a photo in the refreshing rain.

'The beginning,' I say.

It is still early when we arrive back at the surf club the next day. I'm ready to face the world again.

I groan when I see Nina is back, too.

She walks straight for me. I brace myself. How much will it hurt if she punches me? Instead, she embraces me in a hug. 'I'm sorry. I acted like I did.'

'I hope you are ok,' I say.

'You too. I heard what happened.'

'Does everyone know?' I ask, panicked.

'No, just Ryder, Alex and I.'

'Good.'

'I'll tell Petra and Rose too.'

We have a campfire that night.

'These campfires remind me of Camp Te ao mārama,' I say, cooking some damper on the fire.

'I love it there,' Ryder adds.

We are all getting to know each other, and we come from all over the islands, country and city, yet one thing we have in common is that we've all stayed at an environmentally friendly camp in the Waitakere ranges. The other thing is that we all love the beach.

Cody sits next to me the whole time with his arm around my waist. We are finally out as a couple. However, no one seems surprised. As the sun is about to set, the sky is lit up with a bright rainbow. New beginnings. We pack up and run inside just before the rain arrives.

The City

The next day, there is more harmony in the group. As the lifesavers had all had to swap to cover us when we were missing, it is now like one large group of eighteen instead of little clicks of groups. Glad to say that our 5-day shift was easy, no dramas, a few saves, and I still have my little 12-year-old stalker. But that I can handle. Cody and I stay on two days of our weekend to cover some of the people who had worked for us. After one more shift, we are heading off to his place.

'I'm an only child. Mum and Dad are both top in their field—doctors—and I was raised by a string of nannies, so there is no love in my place like there is yours.' He gives me background as we arrive at Cody's place late afternoon. It's double the drive time from the beach than my place is.

'Showing off, are we?' I tease as Cody gives me the lowdown on his family.

'No, not at all. I am embarrassed more so after seeing your family. I never wanted for any physical thing, but I never had a family life. No aunties and uncles, brothers, or sisters. Not complaining, and never cared until I saw how amazing your extended family is. If we ever have a working bee, as James and Vanessa did, no one would be there from my side. Which is why I'm glad we are starting now,' he says.

'I'm showing you where I'm from, more or less, the apartment. You may see my parents a little, and meet my favourite childhood nanny, Ana, but there's no heart and soul like your place.'

Cody's apartment building is taller than any building I've seen before today. It is a five-minute walk from the hospital and a three-minute walk from the University. Plus, thankfully, it's only ten minutes from where I'll be studying on Wednesdays and Thursdays.

'So, when you are here, you do nothing but study?'

Final Week

Together, Cody and I drive back to the surf club. It is our final week. Summer is almost over.

Each night, we have a bonfire. And each night, Cody has his arm around me.

He walks me to my dorm room and kisses me good night. We run together in the mornings, and it's even more perfect now.

A few times, we sneak away and kiss in the dunes, and this is where we are on our second to last day.

Cody's kissing is getting more intense again. He is on top of me, and his hands explore my body.

'Am I frustrating you?' I ask him.

'No, you could never,' he stops and leans on his elbow, looking at me.

'You want to do more, though, don't you?'

'Well yeah, sorry,' he says. 'But I won't, and I'm happy to wait. But I dream of this every night,' he says, his fingertips drawing circles on my stomach, 'But remember, when I am at home, I am a study geek. Most people think I am a virgin. I'm not, but I have only done it once, and I regret it. I don't think that's as good as it gets, and I'm happy to wait. I know it will be even better with you. You know I love you, right?' he says. 'I want to see you as much as I can and call you when I can't. I am not a phone person, but I need you. I need to keep in touch with you.'

'You also have a lot of studies, don't you?' I say.

'A lot,' he agrees.

'I can come to your place and lie next to you while you study, but I like sleeping next to you. Can we share your bed from now on?' I ask him, going red.

'Any time you want,' he grins at me. 'How will I focus on study if you are beside me?'

'I'm hoping I could stay with you Wednesday nights; you study, and I'll bake. Then when I go home, you can eat my baking and think of me.'

'You think I won't be thinking of you?' he asks. 'I want to stay beside you tonight. Want to crash in the clubhouse?'

'Yes,' I say. 'I love waking up in your arms.'

We get up and walk back to the club.

As we arrive, Nina comes up to us. We are holding hands, but when we stop walking, Cody puts his arms around me.

Ryder comes running over, sensing his sister is about to do something.

'I just want to say that I have been watching you. Sorry, I see now our relationship was either in my mind or me manipulating you. You never acted the way you do with Sandra around me.' Her eyes give away how she really feels. Poor Nina.

'Sorry,' Cody says. 'I wanted to focus on studying and didn't want a girlfriend, but I love Sandra and can't be away from her.'

'You love her?' she asks.

'Yes. I love how she's not afraid to get her hands dirty, and she's kind to others. On the first day I met her, she lost a race to help a scared little boy. I have never met anyone like her.'

My face burns with delight.

'Are you sure she's not with you because you are going to be a doctor?' Nina asks him.

'No,' he laughs, pulling me closer. 'She's only just found out about that, and she is bringing much more into this relationship than I am. With her, I get a lifestyle I never thought I'd have. Four crazy brothers who treat me like their own, and I don't only love her, but I love her whole family, the farm and horses, and even the run-down house we are fixing together. I hope that will be our house one day.'

Wow, I didn't know he felt like that, but that's how I feel.

'Dude, you got it bad.' Ryder pats him on the back.

'So bad, and I want to sleep next to her tonight, so want to arrange a camp out?'

'I like the way you think,' Ryder says.

He looks over at Alex.

'I like Alex, not planning my future with her, but she's so good,' Ryder says, raising his eyebrows.

I feel bad I'm not putting out. Alex is already.

'Hey,' Cody whispers, 'I am glad we are waiting; I promise it's worth waiting for, plus we are playing the long game,' and he kisses me.

We go back, set up camp in the clubhouse, and stroll over to the bonfire.

'I am going to miss you so much,' Cody says many, many times between kisses.

Epilogue

J ust under a year later, I stand waiting at the front door, all fidgety.

'Chill out,' Tony laughs at me.

Finally, I hear gravel under wheels. It's James and his new wife coming home. I feel my whole body droops as Tony and James laugh at me.

They are so loud; I miss the next set of wheels on the gravel. I look up, and he is there. No doubt wondering why half of my brothers are laughing at me, and I'm flushed.

I run over to him, and he picks me up as I wrap my legs around him, and he sits me on the car bonnet, kissing me hard.

'Calm down, the olds will see you,' my brothers tease us.

I slide off the car, and hand in hand, we walk to the house. My brothers hug Cody, but he comes straight back to me after. As he does, the rest of my family arrive.

After Cody has said 'hi' to everyone and I pack my bag, we farewell them all and get in his car.

It surprises me when we don't leave but drive to our house. We've fixed the roof, and it's all weathertight now.

'I have a gift from Ana,' Cody says as we pull up. 'She's been going to second-hand trade shops looking for us.'

'She's amazing.' I smile.

Cody pops open the boot and takes out some pavers. I help him. We stack them at the front of our house, and then he holds my hand as we walk inside.

'Any excuse?' I tease him.

'Any excuse,' he agrees with his eyebrows jigging.

A few months ago, we'd finished the bedroom and begged Mum and Dad to let us camp there for the night. We promised we wouldn't get into mischief. That was, of course, the night I lost my virginity, and ever since then, any chance we can get alone, we take it.

Thirty minutes later, we drive to the surf trials, and I say to Cody. 'What if I don't get in?'

'What if I don't?' he says.

'You will,' I assure him.

'As will you.'

'Hey, I've got some big news – I just got accepted into Unitec, I'll be studying interior design.' I grin.

'Perfect – why didn't you tell me?'

'I wanted to tell you in the car.'

'Fair enough. I can't wait to spend more time with you in the city.'

He turns off the main road, and we head to our beach. We enjoy a quick surf, as we are alone.

We do more in the dunes this time.

A few hours later, when we arrive at the surf club, we go our separate ways. I speak to the people I know but don't see Cody for a while.

I register, and again, he is a leader.

This time, I'm at the front and the first person he chooses.

Ryder chooses Alex, who is next to me. They haven't seen each other for nine months, but pick up right where they left off.

We go for a swim in our group, and a boy hits on me. Cody laughs. But then comes over.

'Sorry, she's spoken for,' he says, slipping his arm around me.

I see some girls watching him, and they talk when they see him touch me. So I turn and kiss him.

'Not here, love,' he says. 'But later, I want more.' He kisses my cheek.

He always does – some geek he is.

'Oh my gosh, does the hot leader like you?' a girl skips over to me and asks.

'I hope so. We have a house together,' I say, grinning.

How's that for stamping my man?

The next day on the beach, I compete hard, proving that I'm not chosen just because of my boyfriend. I show everyone that I deserve to be there and am the best at every trial I have.

Cody rewards my efforts in the dunes after the sun has set.

The End.

Acknowledgements

My team, Anna McKersey, Melissa Guyan, Val Carpenter, Melodie Lindsay, Vicki Arnott, Sonya Wilson

My readers, Ruby Sewell. Ashley Lindsay, James Angus, Kane Meredith, Sam Everett

My critique crew, Jess, Jade, Kara Claire, Nic, Sarah, Ashley, Mayur, Kynan, Shan and Tremaine.

My rocks, Tonchi, Marco, Lucas, Frankie, Mum, Diana and Glen and my Pram Fam XXX

My sanity, Tania, Janelle, Julie, Kim, Cinnamon, Anna, Casie, Beca and Liz

Sue Carpenter

Sue is a Junior Fiction and Young Adult Author.

She doesn't want her readers to need a dictionary to fall into her imaginary worlds. Sue is not ready to grow up yet and keeps her mind young by writing for children and spending time with her three sons. To find more of Sue's work follow her on Instagram susieleenz

Other titles by Sue Carpenter

The Black Manor

Belinda's uncle has taught her everything she knows about animals but when he suddenly dies, has he taught her enough to be able to run his pet business? Belinda suspects her uncle's staff are up to more than just breeding parrots so now she has to learn to care for new animals. Caged kiwis and strange sounding boxes have Belinda on edge. What secrets are the staff hiding; are her family and animals safe?

Lavender and Pearls

Jackie and her brother Hayden are sent to stay at their eccentric Aunt's Antique shop in New Zealand, where they discover a magical secret. When her family members start to go missing, Jackie must venture into fantastical and dangerous new lands to save them. Will Jackie rescue her family? And what secrets will she discover along the way?

The Dramatic Bubble

Kenzie wants to focus on her school exams with no distractions, but cupid, COVID and the government have other ideas. Will the Catholic boy be a distraction for her, or the only thing that holds her together as her family life collapses?